The Greatest Story Ever Told

NewCon Press Novellas

The Greatest Story Ever Told

Una McCormack

NewCon Press
England

First published in the UK by NewCon Press
41 Wheatsheaf Road, Alconbury Weston, Cambs, PE28 4LF
March 2018

NCP 143 (limited edition hardback)
NCP 144 (softback)

10 9 8 7 6 5 4 3 2 1

ISBN:

978-1-910935-67-5 (hardback)
978-1-910935-68-2 (softback)

Cover art by Jim Burns
Cover layout by Ian Whates

Minor editorial meddling by Ian Whates
Text layout by Storm Constantine

Part I

AUTUMN

One

I remember it was autumn, not that you'd have known it. The heat had gone on and on and everyone was right fucked off with the whole thing. Every day you'd look out at the sky and think – bastard stars, when is there going to be some bastard rain around here? And it didn't come, it just didn't come and you started to think that it would never come again.

So that was what it was like. Simmering. And at the back of your mind you was thinking: this is what it's going to be like from now on. It'll never be wet again and all there'll be forever is the rocks and the stone and the dry world and the simmering shimmering sky and not even the stars can help.

I was stuck in the kitchen. I was always stuck in the kitchen. I had been for years and I was going to be for years, and then I'd die and turn back into dirt, and that was all there was to it. I'd started trotting around on my little legs, fetching and carrying, and as I got bigger I got more and more dumped on me. First up in the morning and last to bed at night and hardly a moment to myself in between. You don't get eighty dance-fighters fed and watered without a lot of hard work, and most of that was mine. I'm not saying Kallanish shirked, mind you, and I'd certainly never have said that in her hearing, all I'm saying is that Kal was good at handing out jobs, and I was the one that got most of them.

You know about the dance-fighters, yeah? Surely everyone knows about the dance-fighters, even if they speak with a little more fear in their voice than they did back in the day. Back then, it was all anyone ever talked about – and I mean everyone, free-folk and hand alike – and it was where most people put their money. You scuffled around for a piece or two to get you into the pit at the flicks, and crammed yourself up against everyone else, and listened to the band thump out the music as the dance whirled on. The dance-fighters made the flicks. It was all everyone wanted to see, really – not the weepies or even the journeys up and out into the stars, but those beautiful strong figures whirling and twisting and turning, like they were powerful, like they were free.

Do I have to say how much I loved watching them? Everyone loved watching them, didn't they? That's why they made Battiaire so much money and I bet she was up and running again in no time with a new troupe. I tell you, by all the stars in the heaven, you might think you've seen them on the flicks but you haven't seen anything till you've seen them in the flesh like the rich did. Like I did. No, I did, really I did, all the time. Not that I ever got close, mind you, I'll admit that. There was a back door in the scullery, down where I did the pans, and there was a metal grille in the door and sometimes when my feet were killing me I'd stop for a minute or two – not long, mind, Kallanish would have my bastard hide – and I'd stand and watch them train.

They'd turn and twist and dodge and dive – I tell you what, though, more of it's choreographed than you'd think, so if you did ever put some cash on them you were being robbed, but oh my! Still it was so beautiful! I saw them all that way – Darish, Ettelish, even Nor, right at the end of her career before her back snapped. And yes, of course I saw Seffish. That's the point of this story – haven't you worked that out yet? And I saw Crith too, although I am willing to bet you every piece you've got there in your bastard pocket that you don't remember that name. But they always came as a pair. Seffish and Crith: two parts of a whole, and, yes, you loved one or you loved the other, and you swore at the other side and called them idiots, but the fact is that neither of them was anything without the other. That was the problem, in the end. Neither was the same without the other.

So, yes, there I'd stand, in that little hot dark room, full of steam and grease, standing on tip-toes to look through the bars and watch them train. Not for long, mind. Soon enough I'd hear Kallanish yelling from upstairs or clattering downstairs and I'd jump back to my scrubbing pretty bastard quick. Kallanish didn't lay her hands on me that often but bastard stars she knew how to hit so it hurt. But I loved them, I loved them all, and I loved Seffish best. Strongest, fastest, toughest, smartest. As far as I was concerned she was a goddess, or the nearest us poor bastards will ever get to see.

So. That day. I'd been let out that morning by Kal, off the leash you might say, although it was on an errand, and while it was tempting to fuck off for a while and worry about what would happen later, the fact was the day was too fucking hot. I thought about slipping into the flicks, but I didn't have a spare piece, of course, I never did, and I could hardly slip in unnoticed with a bastard sack of veggies on my back, now could I? Besides, it would stink in there, all the sweaty bodies crushed together in the pit, getting hotter and hotter as the fight went on. What I wanted was to nip down to the waterside, but it was too far away. So I thought I may as well head back to the compound, and maybe Kal would take pity on me and let me sit in the shade for a bit. Fat chance, but hope springs eternal.

I didn't exactly hurry, mind you. The way back to the compound was uphill, no avoiding that, so I took my time, and kept to the quiet streets, and halfway there I came out onto the street on the ridge with the railings, where you can stand and look down across the city and the road out into the plain and, far in the distance, the old smoky mountain. Look the other way and you'd see the red sands, and then the water with the little boats bobbing about, off on journeys I never thought to take. There it was, the old south town of Capallaire, the only place I'd ever known, and beyond was... Well, whatever I could imagine. Because as far as I knew, that morning, there was no chance I'd ever get past the city walls or even, to be honest, much beyond that stinking scullery, so I might as well make up whatever I liked.

The houses sweated under my eyes. It was a big celebration the following day, one of those festivals the free-folk have to their strange gods. They're a superstitious lot, the masters, make a big deal of their gods, always trying to placate them like they felt guilty about something or other. Us... we're not fooled by that stuff. Oh they try, yes, they try – they like to make us learn their chants and prayers and parables, but I've never met one of us who takes a word of it seriously. Oh yes, yes, when the masters are there, it's all lowered eyes and soft, soft voices, but behind closed doors? I'd better not say. You'd be shocked, I think, at the way we laughed at those old gods. And besides – what was a feast day to us, anyway? More work, less sleep, and certainly no feast. Hard to celebrate that kind of thing.

So everyone was busy, despite the heat. I admit I may have dozed off for a while, and then a sort of humming noise, a buzzing overhead, woke me up. I looked up and saw an iron-bird. I know they're everywhere now, but didn't see them much in those days, and even as you looked at them and thought, "Well, if they can do that kind of thing, there's not much hope we'll slip our yokes…" you still had to admire what they could do, those masters of ours, how clever they were, how they made things work for them. There's beauty in iron, I don't deny it. But I don't want to feel it.

The 'bird flew off down the coast. I got up, stretched, shook myself, and hiked that bloody sack up again onto my back. I tottered off uphill, slow but steady, and got back to the compound just after the sun passed the highest point.

I knew at once that something was off. The back gate was slightly open, for one thing, and that's never the case. I often wondered later if Kallanish had sent me off on purpose and was banking on me taking the piss and staying out all day. Half of me thinks I should be grateful that she wanted me away from trouble while the other half is angry that she would have fucked off and left me there all alone. So what, you say, but – well, I had no one else, did I? I was hers and she was mine.

Carefully, I came through the gate. Everything was very quiet. Usually you'd hear some noise from the big kitchen above where I worked, but today there was nothing. I dumped my sack by the back door, and I was about to go down the little stone steps to my dungeon when something moved me to try the back door. It opened, easily. Inside, the kitchen was empty. Nobody at work.

Someone here, I thought, was going to get the mother of all beltings. I didn't want it to be me.

Still, I tiptoed through, past the pots and pans and ovens. There was nothing cooking. Another clue. I went out through the door, and down the passageway. I'd never really been this far into the compound before – not for the likes of me. I guessed my way towards the yard where the livestock was kept, and I found the door that led out there. There I saw Kal, and the rest of the kitchen hands with her, and beside her, back to me, was a figure in a cloak and hood. There was a few more standing around like this. Funny clothes for this weather.

"Hey, Kal," I said. "What's going on?"

The figure in the cloak nearest Kal spun around, and I got a good look at the face.

Seffish. Beautiful Seffish, here in our back yard.

"It's only that bastard kid from the kitchen," she said, and bastard stars I wouldn't have thought she'd ever have known me but turns out I was famous. "The one that hangs around the back door."

They all started to laugh. They were all looking at me now, and I could see who they were under the hoods – Seffish, yes, and Crith too, and half-a-dozen of the others. I thought I had a pretty good idea now what was going on. The fighters were loose, and the kitchen-hands were helping them, and oh my Kal did you really want me to miss all this? What was your plan, eh? That you'd go free and I'd stay scrubbing?

One of the fighters stepped forwards, lifted me up, and carried me over to Kal.

"Hey," I said, "get your paws off me."

She laughed at me, and she didn't let go either. So I bit her on the arm. She wasn't laughing so much then, I can tell you that.

"Fucking little bastard," she said, and got ready to belt me, but before she could Seffish had hold of her hand.

"No need," she said, and then she did it. She smiled at me – me, Iss from the kitchens, with her ratty hair and her greasy face, and she said, "You like watching the dance, don't you?"

Didn't know where to put myself. "Yeah," I said, sticking my chin. "It's all right."

"Show some respect or I'll belt you," said Kal.

"You'd better bastard not," I said. "I'm free now."

And Seffish laughed – her beautiful big laugh, like a bell.

And that was why they took me with them. Us hands don't believe in luck, but still – I was their mascot.

The Story of the Hand Who Sank into the Ground

This is the rock, the rock of the world, upon whose bones everything rests.

Once upon a time there was a child who lived in the care of seven sisters. They loved her greatly, and so they worked her hard and expected much of her. As she grew, she watched what they did, and learned from them, and when she was big enough she went out to the land with them, and she worked the hardest and the best, picking and sifting and spinning. She was the best of hands, loved and cherished.

One day, a child came to her in turn, as bright as stars and sweet as water. The hand loved the child, in the way hands do, teaching it all she had learned and cherishing her in secret. And the child grew and prospered in her care, surpassing even her. The hand knew that a child as bright and as sweet as this one would be desired, so she hid her away, under cover, and would not let her out into the land.

But children do not bend to the will of others, and this child was no different. She was curious about what lay beyond the bounds that had been set for her, and one night, when everyone was sleeping, she slipped outside. And she saw the stars in their bright hard glory high up in the cold heavens, and she felt the soft rain on her cheeks, sweet and precious, and she could not help but laugh out loud for the sheer joy of living.

But the birds, hearing her laughter, looked around with their sharp eyes, and they saw the child as bright as stars and sweet as water, and they wanted her. They gathered together in a huge, dark cloud, and they planned and schemed, and when their plans were made, they sent one of their number to find the child and bring her to them.

Each night, the bird tapped upon the child's window, and sang to her, *Come away with me... Come away with me...* But the child, who had listened carefully to all her lessons, shook her head and hid beneath the covers, and tried not to listen. But the bird sang ever more sweetly, sang of stars and rivers and mountains, and at last the child could not resist the song any longer, and she threw back the covers, and ran outdoors, and cried to the bird that she would follow wherever it led. But as soon as she cried out loud, she realised her mistake, because high above the stars were blotted out by a great black cloud, moving quickly. The birds were gathering overhead, and when they saw the child they swept down from the sky. The child screamed and begged for mercy, but the birds seized her, and carried her away.

The scream pierced the night, and woke the hand, and she knew at once what had happened. The child – the precious child, cherished in secret and beyond measure, as bright as stars and sweet as water – was in danger. She ran outside, but she was far, far too late, and the last she saw of the child was her small hands, reaching downwards, as the birds stole her away. And the hand cried out, a sound as terrible as a cornered beast, a cry so great it shook the rock of the world to its foundations. The seven sisters, hearing, came flying to her, and, seeing what had happened, they took her in their arms, and stroked her hair, and told her to forget the child, because the birds do not return what they have taken.

"Listen to us," they pleaded with her, "and learn this lesson, the hardest one of all: put her from your mind, forget her, and perhaps one day there will be another child as bright as the stars and sweet as water. But this one is gone, never to return."

But the hand would not listen to them, and she felt her heart heavy like stone, and she bent to the ground and placed her palms down flat, and she rocked to and fro, and as she rocked she made this promise: that she would never forget her precious child, and she would never leave the world until her child was returned to her, and until that day she would not pick or sift or spin, but only wait and weep.

And as she crouched there, crying and making this promise, her tears fell upon the rock of the world, and upon her hands, and a change began to come over her. Her hands hardened, and her arms and then her whole body turned to stone, and became part of the rock of the world. The grass cloaks her, and the flowers crown her, and the starlight caresses her, and the water keeps her clean.

But the birds never dare come near her.

And you can see her still, the hand that sank into the ground, because she is the rock of the world around us, and everything rests upon her bones, and she is always there and cannot escape her promise, and before she turned completely into stone she swore that one day she would rise up and the whole land would follow her. When that day comes, we will rock the foundations of the world, and break our fetters, and catch the birds and cage them. And we will take back our children, as bright as stars and sweet as water.

We all know this story. We have whispered it to each other ever since history began, when the masters descended upon us like a cloud of pecking birds, and first stole the children from us. We have taught it to each other and repeated it down the years, like a threat, like a promise.

Two

I pieced together what had happened. The fighters had ganged up and taken the compound, and the kitchen hands had joined them and opened up the gates. Well, I wondered why nobody had ever thought of doing that before, and I wondered why they'd decided to do it now. Batiaire, that bastard, they trussed up and locked in a cupboard – lucky escape, I'd say. If there were any justice in this old hard world (and I can tell you how little justice there is), then Batiaire would be strung up on an old forked log, or dropped into the sea. Some people make their fortune through the pain of others, and don't seem to learn why they shouldn't. I don't know why the dancers and the kitchen-hands showed her mercy. Perhaps that was our mistake from the start.

Soon enough we were out on the street. Well, at that point I didn't know half of what was going on, so I didn't reckon on us lasting past nightfall, or a day or two at the outside, and I'm pretty sure most of the rest of us didn't either. I think most of us thought that this was our one day of freedom, and that we'd be lucky to see tomorrow's sunset. So we were going to enjoy it while it lasted. There was a lot of drinking, a lot of what Kallanish called 'insubordination', although how she'd ended up the boss of us I didn't exactly know. But there it was: for all her strength and prowess, for all she was clearly our leader, our hero, the one that we loved most, Seffish listened to Kallanish, and followed her advice in more or less everything. Crith was always second. That wasn't a problem at first. And then it was. A very big problem.

Well, you were wise, on the whole, if you listened to Kallanish, because the bastard thing was that she usually made good sense. First thing she wanted done was find the town's armoury. There were a couple of tense moments when someone free thought they could simply step in front of us and tell us to stand down, do what we were told, and go back to our work, but it quickly became clear to the town-folk that wasn't going to happen. We were out now. We weren't taking orders any more. One of the dancers had brought a whip, one of the big ones that Batiaire used on their legs and feet in training, and she let in loose at the one who was trying to order us about. How we all laughed, watching her hop. And the gang she'd brought with her were soon sent on their way.

I got to admit I enjoyed watching them run. I know what they say, the masters: that our pleasure at this goes to show what they've always said, that how we're animals really; that it proves how we need to be curbed, but let me tell you that if you'd been kicked or pushed or stepped on as much as we have, you'd kick back too. Did nobody ever think about that? Once or twice it got really nasty, and I thought one of the freefolk was done for, but, for now, people obeyed orders, and they didn't go in for the kill.

We got to the heart of the town. It was all dressed up for the festival, of course, bright garish colours. Banners hanging up between buildings, and a few of the statues of the town god were already out, ready for the procession the day after. A few of us started kicking that over, pulling things down. One of the statues toppled down with a crash, and a cheer went up from us, and we heard a few free gasp at the blasphemy. Crith soon put a stop to all this.

"Leave it," she ordered. "They can have their fun tomorrow, if they can find anyone to do the work for them."

Outside the armoury, half-a-dozen half-grown guards were standing in front of the doors, clutching nervously onto batons. Whoever had ordered them here hadn't even armed them properly. None of them looked very old; kids from artisan families, I'd guess, the children of the free poor who are always first up against the wall when the real masters want to get some extra killing done. Oh my stars, they were well out of their league in the face of our dancers. A few quick flicks and kicks and they were down. There was no sign of anyone else, so we just helped ourselves to what was in there. I often think about how easily we won there. Did we never realise how much power we had, how much strength? Had we come to believe everything they always said about us – that we were lazy, that we needed orders to do anything complicated? I saw none of that. I saw focus, and determination, and a clear goal. And the masters weren't prepared. We had caught them on the hop. They weren't ready for something this organised.

Anyway, that was how our troupe got armed. And, well, yes, it was pretty clear to me by now that this wasn't simply a riot. This wasn't opportunistic. There was a plan going on behind all this. And since I wanted to know what, I stuck as close to Kallanish as I possibly could, a habit I kept up over the next few months. She wasn't daft; didn't miss what I was doing, she didn't miss anything, old Kal. As Seff and Crith oversaw the distribution of the weapons, I slid up next to her. She was looking up at the sky, and I looked up too.

High overhead, I saw an iron-bird circling, round and round, over the town. I heard the *chop-chop-chop* of its engine and I shivered in the heat. Then I felt a hand on my shoulder. Kallanish. She'd seen me looking.

"You know what that means?" she said.

"Yeah," I said. "They're watching us. They'll be coming for us."

"So what should we do?"

I gaped at her. "Why're you asking me, Kal?"

"Why're you not answering, Iss?"

Her hand upon my shoulder was firm, I realised, but not unkind. I knew when Kal was warming up to giving me a belting; knew it better than most things. Slowly, I said, "Me, I'd get out of here. Get some trucks, get on the move. Find the others." I eyed her, cannily. "There *are* others, aren't there?"

A smile touched her lips. Kal's smile was chipped from the rock of the world. It's almost scarier than her hand.

"Then definitely," I said. "Get away from here as fast as we could. There's strength in numbers, isn't there?"

"You not liking having the run of the town, Iss?"

"I'm loving it. And everyone else is loving it, too much maybe. But they're coming, aren't they? And if they find us here they won't leave a single one of us alive. Not the dancers, not you, not even me. They'll string up every last one of us and leave us to the birds."

As if she didn't know that. Her grip on my shoulder tightened, then she let go and shooed me on my way. "Go and make yourself useful," she said.

"Doing what?"

"Get some grub organised."

I didn't muck around. There's a time to take the piss, and there's a time to do what you're told, and spotting the difference is almost the first lesson a hand learns.

We set off before sunset. There were more than a few complaints, but Kallanish soon stopped that. I don't know – people just wanted to savour the freedom for a while, didn't they? But I knew why. Time to get moving. Don't hang around for them to come and get us before we'd even had a chance to get properly started.

By this time we had a few trucks – and we'd picked up followers from other hands from around the town. Crith wasn't sure about this, and I could see that Seffish was almost persuaded, but Kallanish put her foot down. I watched them, three heads together, arguing in soft voices. That was something I'd get to see a lot of over the next while.

"We shouldn't bring them," said Crith. "They'll slow us up –"

"So what do we do with them?" said Kal. "Send them back? They'll be strung up outside the walls –"

"I'm not saying send them back," said Crith. "But they're one more thing to worry about. I say we get to where we're going, quick as we can, and they can make their own way –"

"Look at them," said Kal. "Look at the state of them. There's kids and oldies there. You want them to walk? Half of them will drop dead on the way, never mind what would happen if the masters catch up with them. Seffy," she said, appealing to the third, who had been standing there, silent, and listening. "They deserve to be free as much as the rest of us. If we leave them behind, we're no better than the masters."

"Now hang on a minute," said Crith, "I'm not having that!"

"True though," said Kal. "Isn't it?"

"All I mean is, slowing us down makes us an easier target. We give them a truck, give them supplies, tell them to come and join us. But if we're wiped out before we've even started, we're no use to anyone, are we?"

I could see Seffish thinking it through. Hard choices. Nobody wants to have to make them. "We'll take them with us," she said at last, and Kal nodded. *Good, good.* "I'm sorry, Crith. I get your point. But there's little ones. Old ones. Who's to look after them, if not us?"

And Crith agreed, and not in bad spirit, although I could see her point, and I could see why she was worried. But we all travelled together, down the dusty road.

At last, far from the town, we stopped, and camped. The stars came up. You'll hear a lot about the stars in this story. I like the stars. Who doesn't? You're a hard old soul if you don't look at the stars and wonder. I like stories about the stars best of all. Here's one, let's start with this one. I heard a story once about how the way the stars stood at your birth told you what your life would be like, what kind of person you'd be. The masters, the richer ones – or so I'd heard, because I didn't exactly hob-nob with that exalted sort – used to pay good money to people to plot out the stars at the moment of their birth, so that they could see what the future would hold.

Honestly, how did these people ever get to lord it over us? It's all rubbish, isn't it? Stars can't do that. Stars can't control you. Not really. But that's not how stories work, is it? Stories might not tell the actual truth, but they're trying to tell you some kind of truth. And sometimes they have to disguise themselves so that the wrong people don't hear. Sometimes you have to work out what they're trying to tell you, behind the disguise and the smokescreen. Here's what I think that story is trying to tell us. Not that everything you are is written in the stars, but that where you're born can set you up for life if you're born high up enough, or else it can drag you down, if you're born in the gutter. That story is saying – yes, things aren't fair, but it's not your fault. It's not because of you, it's because of other things. So maybe, just maybe, those things ought to change. Not you.

See? You couldn't tell that story out loud, could you? Imagine one of the free-folk hearing. They'd have your tongue out. So you disguise it, and you say, oh yeah, the stars control us and we can't do anything about that, and what that means is that where you're born is the whole of who you are and you have to suck it up. And the free-folk, hearing that, like it, because it tells them that they're great. But if you listen to the story, really listen, it's got another little message inside, just for you and people like you.

I like that. I like it when stories do that. And I know for a fact that where and how you're born can change. Change utterly.

We were about a week on the road, the weakest in the trucks, with the food and water, and the rest walking. I walked a lot of the way, although sometimes, at the end of the day, Kal bundled me up on the truck despite my complaints.

"Shut up and sit down," she'd say, and she always got it right. She always spotted when I was getting light-headed, and stumbling. The days were still hot.

The countryside we passed through was tired. A few abandoned homesteads here and there, not much, but we took what pickings we could find. This was old land, rocky, used up, the fields dried in the late-starting autumn, the streams thin. At one point the road crossed the old canal, sluggish and low. We picked up a few more people here and there, hands from farms to the north who had got the message somehow, and decided to try their luck with us. We weren't bothered by the masters – except each evening, I'd see it, and Kal would see it too, I knew: the 'bird in the sky, circling.

I wondered what they had planned for us, the masters, and whether they'd get to us before we reached out destination. By this point, I knew where we were heading. Where else, really? We were off to the smoky mountain.

The Story of the Smoky Mountain

Here's a story I heard a lot when I was small. Kal used to tell it all the time, so I wouldn't get too big for my boots, I guess. You'd hear it from the masters sometimes too, and the free-folk, when they wanted to remind you not to be so bastard cheeky and remember what your purpose was in life. It's the story about the smoky mountain, that same smoky mountain where we were heading, and where I was going to have the first real adventure of my so-far boring life.

The story starts with one of their gods. I've said already that they like their gods, which is funny for people who like to invent stuff, but perhaps it's because they set so much store in some people being better than others, and then they worry that maybe our there are beings more powerful than them. I don't know. I don't believe that kind of rubbish.

So here is a story about one of their gods, who was a smith. Yes, this god made things, as if she was a hand. But – and this is funny for a god – she wasn't very good at it. One of the other gods was jealous, and put a curse on her, so that everything she tried was broken in some way, flawed. And one day, as her latest effort broke around her in pieces, she lifted up her hammer and threw it across the land, cursing her desire to make and build, and swearing she would never use her hands again.

Well, it fell with a mighty bump, ever so big, and left a huge crater where it landed. Little shards of bright stone scattered all round and glittered in the hot sun. And the sky god, the master of masters, looked at this, and at the smith-god, bubbling and boiling with anger, and she leaned down from her seat amongst the stars and breathed upon the bright stones.

As the smith-god watched, the stones came to life, and began to collect up all the rocks and stones around, and fill up the crater. When the crater was full up, they didn't stop, but carried on, carried on lifting stones and rocks, and the smith-god realised that they were doing what she had been trying to do, which was build a mountain. So she sat at the side, and she pictured what she was trying to build, and somehow these builders seemed to know what she wanted, and they got on with the job. They acted like her hands. But because they weren't cursed in the way the smith-god was, they were able to build properly.

Well, it took a long time, because it was a bastard lot of hard work, but eventually the mountain was there, standing high and proud above the plain. The smith-god gave her orders, and they stopped their work and stood back. Then the smith-god walked to the mountain, and she cupped it between her hands, to warm it, and the whole thing sprang to life. Smoke billowed from the top, and then the hot rocks flowed, and the smith clapped her hands together in glee. It was exactly what she'd wanted to make. When the lava finished flowing, the plain beneath was full of good soil, and the god of good things saw the hands standing by, and told them to work the land and build the shelters, and get everything ready. When everything was done, the sky-god took a handful of stars, and sprinkled them on the earth, and they became the masters.

"Here is the world we have made for you," the sky-god said, "everything is ready, and now you are here you must lead your fullest lives, your best lives. We have filled the fields and the waters, and we have left you servants, so that you can think and they can work."

And that's how the masters and the hands came into being. They are stars and we are stones. They are here to think and we are here to work. And that's the end of that.

I think about this story a lot. Some stories, they're trying to tell you why things are the way they are so that you think, "Oh, well, there's nothing I can do about that." And I think what this story is trying to tell us – the hands – is that the world is split between people who think things, and people who make things, and that the makers are there to do the work so that the thinkers are free to think, and that's the way the world works, and, on the whole, it's a very good way of going about things.

What do you think of that? I reckon it's a load of bastard rubbish. Making is thinking; thinking is making. It doesn't take half a brain to work that one out.

There's a flaw in this story, did you spot it? Yes, that's right. If the smith-god had been cursed, and everything she built was flawed in some way, then how did the mountain send up flames the way she wanted? There's a simple answer to that, isn't there?

No? You don't see it? You don't get it? You have to look between the lines of what a story's telling you, remember. You have to look into its cracks and see what's there.

We built the mountain. We brought the mountain to life.

We are the rock of the world. We are its foundations. Everything rests on us and without us there is nothing.

Three

Two days from the mountain we met Oenith and her band.

They were from a farm – one of the big farms – to the north-west, deep in the country and away from the coast. Flat and dry. They were hard, like the land they had worked; hard like rock, and not kind. They recognised our dancers as fighters, and so did not challenge Seffish in her leadership, but at the same time you could sense the hard contempt in which they held all of us – town-dwellers, soft, with no real clue of what life was like for those who worked the countryside. But we did know. We knew because it was an ever-present threat. Lazy? Aging? Too much spirit or wit? You'll be sent to the farms.

The masters – the rich ones – talk a lot about the countryside, and you hear their pride in their ownership of land, and a house on the land, and grounds around it. They travel out from the cities to their houses there, dragging half their households with them, and there they gather, and entertain each other, and there's sport and plenty of food and drink, and I don't doubt there's a murder or two as well, if the flicks are anything to go by. They like to peek inside these country houses, at the flicks. That way of life isn't so bad, I suppose, and when the masters aren't there, which is most of the time, I should think it's pretty fine, if dull. Imagine being stuck out there in the middle of nowhere, only a big house to rattle round, and maybe the odd barge on the canal if you were lucky, and nothing to do except when the masters chose to visit, when you hardly saw your bed from running round with all the work to do. Give me the town any day, even my greasy old dungeon. At least I could get out every so often, sneak into the flicks, or dawdle home and listen to the gossip in the streets.

But the farm Oenith and her gang came from was something very different. No big house there, no kitchen garden to cultivate, or household tasks – these farms were business, and they were run in the way the masters ran all their business: with an eye for profit, and without pity. They were big – field after field that had once been homesteads, now gathered together for efficiency's sake – and there were high fences around them, and we knew that nothing good happened within. People have to be fed, the masters say, and the land needs working properly...

and, well, we're lazy, aren't we? We need proper supervision. Proper motivation.

There were nearly twenty of them, certainly not the whole gang that would have been working that patch of land, and I heard Crith say in passing to Seffish that it must have been a tough fight, getting their freedom from that plantation. Stars, though, they were an ugly bunch, scarred round the wrists and ankles, and sunburned; three of them with eye-patches and four without tongues. They stared at us as if we were the enemy and they'd like to murder us. I wondered at the wisdom of having them along, and, listening in, I gathered Crith thought the same, but she agreed with Kal and Seffish that the extra bodies would be handy in a fight. Once, because this is me I'm talking about and sometimes I can't help myself, I got too close. One of them saw me, and opened her mouth, and I saw where her tongue should have been. I ran like the bastard wind, and heard her wheezing laugh behind me all the way. After that, I kept my distance. Because you could see that they hated us, really, hated our relative freedom and our softer lives, and above all they loathed the children. I don't know. Perhaps because their own had been taken, like in the story, or perhaps because they had never been children themselves. I don't know and I didn't get close enough to ask. They kept themselves to themselves, mostly, talking in their own harsh dialect, which was rubbed down and mean, making their own campfires and cooking at them. But sometimes you felt a hard cold eye upon you, and you shivered in the heat.

Still, there was a fight coming, and so we had to be glad of what we got. There were five hundred raw recruits headed our way, hastily drafted from around the region, and marching towards the mountain as fast as they could. How did I know that? Well, therein lies a tale, although I'll admit it doesn't exactly cover me in glory. You'll have seen how I kept myself close to Kal, not only because she was what I knew best and I knew where I stood with her, but also because that way I always knew what was going on. I had not spent my whole life at the bottom of the pecking order without learning how to tiptoe round the shadows and pass unnoticed. Either you were dodging a job or you were dodging a belting, so it was a good skill to cultivate. So I'd known pretty soon after we'd left town that we were able to send and receive long-casts. I told you there was a plan, didn't I?

All I wanted was a look at the 'caster. I'd never seen one before, although I knew all about them, of course, but I'd never seen one in action. So I thought I'd take a quick peek.

I knew that one of the hands that we'd brought from town was good at tinkering, and that they were looking after the thing, keeping it working, somehow, given the state it was in. And the masters say we can't do thinking. So I waited till late one night, when we were all fed and sleepy, and I slipped off to the truck where they kept it. Lifted up the flap and hopped inside. The 'caster was hidden under a cloth behind a sack of roots.

Well, it wasn't much to look at, I have to say, and I think if I hadn't known what it was I'd have thought it was a bag of bits and bolts, waiting to be scrapped or made useful. But this was our 'caster: the way we got messages from the others; the way we sent message back. Stars. Our whole endeavour, reliant on this pile of shit.

I didn't touch it. I'm not that stupid. I knew what it meant to us, and I wasn't going to be the one who broke it. Someone else could have that dumped on their doorstep. I was half sorry I'd come to look – I'd rather not think about us so dependent on something so crappy. I put the cloth back over it, moved the sack back in front of it, and hopped out of the truck.

Next thing I knew someone had grabbed me by the arm and spun me round.

Kal.

She was spitting mad, and even madder when she saw it was me.

"Iss!" she hissed. "You little bastard! What do you think you're doing?"

"I was just having a look –"

"If you've broken anything I'll kick you off the fucking mountain!"

"I've not broken anything!"

"You're always poking into things that are none of your bastard business!"

"Hey!" I said. "It's my business what's happening, as much as anyone else's."

"It's not your business to go poking around in things we need to keep secret!"

"That?" I pointed back into the truck. "Not the biggest secret round here, is it?"

She looked horrified at that, and I thought: *Oh, you thought it was...*

"Kal, I just made a good guess that's all –"

"Shut up!"

Well, that pissed me off. I was trying to make friends again. I stood my ground and shouted back, "No! I'll not shut up! And don't you think about belting me, Kal, because I'll belt you right back!"

I'll remember that moment long as I live. She looked like I'd done what I'd said and belted her.

"You're not the boss of me now!" I said. "I'm free as you now, you know!" We were nose to nose, eye to eye, her looking like she wanted to murder me. Well, it all got a bit much. I sat down on the hard ground with a bump and burst into tears.

Eventually, with a sigh, she sat down next to me. Close, but not close enough to touch. That was Kal and me all over. "I swear, Iss, one day I am gonna strangle you."

"Rather you didn't, Kal."

"Your arm all right?"

"Yeah. S'pose." I was still sniffling; she'd really yanked my shoulder, the bastard old witch.

She said, "You should have stayed back in town."

"In town?"

"You'd have been safe there."

"No I wouldn't. I'd have caught it with the rest of them when the soldiers arrived."

She glared at me. "What do you mean?"

"You know what I mean. They'll have set an example, won't they? That's why you wanted to let them come along, wasn't it? To save as many as you could. Stop them being strung up."

She didn't answer that. I said, "Do you think they did it, Kal? Do you think they strung them up?"

I had pals back there. People I saw dashing round, doing errands, like me. People who hadn't come with us. What were the masters doing to them now?

Kal stirred the dirt with her heel. She had a different pair of shoes on than she'd always worn, and I wondered where she'd got them from. One of the little empty homesteads we'd passed on the way, I supposed. I wondered who had once owned them and why they had left them behind. Good shoes come along once in a lifetime.

"Look," she said, after a while, "this isn't going to be easy, you know.

It's going to get nastier and there's a good chance we'll not win."

Well, I knew what that meant: that we'd all be captured and killed. Strung up. But I didn't know the other half of it. The other end of the story. "What do you mean by win, Kal?"

She didn't answer right away. She sat head down, chin upon her chest. Her hair had begun to grow, and hung in tight curls around her face. It made her look different; softer, maybe, although you'd be daft to make a mistake about Kal. She was hard as the rock of the world. I guess, looking back, I was grateful for that.

"All I want," she said, at last, "is for us to live in peace."

She leaned towards me, lifting her hand as she did so. I shrunk back: force of habit. But for once she didn't wallop me. She ran her thumb, softly, along the curve of my cheek and jaw. In her eyes I saw a gold glow of something I didn't recognise at first, but then realised was love. You know, I felt angry. I thought: *Why did you never look at me like this before, Kal? Why have you waited till now?* But in my heart I knew the answer: that this world wasn't set up for the likes of us, that it would not hesitate to use us up and drop us in the dirt, and if to keep me alive she had to teach me to be afraid, then she would do that. And, being Kal, she would do it to the best of her ability.

"What's going to happen?" I said.

"I dunno," she said. "But I'm telling you now, Iss – if it starts going wrong, you don't hang around here, yeah? No heroics. I want you on your way. No mucking about."

"All right," I said, although how I was supposed to do that I wasn't sure. How did she think I was going to get past that army, exactly? Fly?

We walked back to where I slept. "Go to bed," she said. I nodded, lay back, and closed my eyes. I heard her walk away, a few steps, and then stop. Watching over me, Kal? I didn't look. I slowed my breathing down so that she thought I had gone to sleep, and waited until I heard her leave. Then I opened my eyes again.

The sky was clear and, oh yes, how beautiful it was. Is there anything like a starry sky to take you out of yourself, to make you feel like your worries aren't going to eat you up, but are something small, something you can manage? Some nights, back in town, I'd not been able to see the stars, because the wind had blown up the dirt from the plain, filling the sky. You couldn't see past it. You couldn't see anything beyond it. And you felt hopeless, like you were trapped, and you'd always be trapped, and there was nothing beyond this world and never could be. I hated nights like that. But tonight was nothing like that. There were the stars, twinkly and bright. I'm not kidding myself: they're not smiling down on you or winking at you or anything daft like that. But they take you out of yourself, don't they? They make you remember that the world went on before you, and it will go on after you, and you had to try your best not to worry too much in between.

The Story of the World Without a Sky

Once upon a time, a very long time after history started, even later than where we are now, there was a world that had got so used up that everyone had to stay inside. Imagine that! A world full of people who could no longer see the sky.

What a place this was, this world without a sky. Perhaps, if you were clever with your hands and your mind, you could build a great ship that would fly to the stars, and then you could look back down at this world, and what marvels and terrors you would see. You would see huge towers, and dark clouds, and bright lights, and oceans of metal, and you would be both amazed and afraid. But you would not see any people, because they were scared of what was outside, where everything was strange and poisoned, and they stayed indoors, in their towers and factories, and tried to forget that there had ever been an outside,

And perhaps if you looked at them carefully, you might decide that they were happy, the people who lived inside without the sky, or perhaps some of them were. Everything was done for them, you see – their food came to them, and their water, and they made machines to do their work for them, or hid away from those of them who still had to work. And they filled their days with flicker screens and bickering, which by and large kept them busy.

But this old world has her own rhythms, and she will not be ignored.

One day, one very much like every other, one of the people who lived without a sky woke up, and got up, and got dressed, and sat in her chair, and turned on her flicker screen to see what had been happening during the night. But the screen didn't work. She shook it, and she thumped it, and she shouted at it, but that didn't do any good, so she stood in the middle of her room – which was a nice room, on the whole, mostly because it was hers, and hers alone – and tried to think about what she should do. But she couldn't think of anything to do, so she thought that the best thing to do was to wait.

She waited, and she waited, and after a while she began to feel very strange. Now, I am sure that you have felt this way, and the stars know that I have felt this way, and we know what it is and what to do, or, at least, how to get by while we're feeling that way, which is hungry. But our friend who lived without a sky had never felt this way before, and at first she thought she was sick, and then she thought she was dying, and although she pressed buttons and rang bells, nobody came. She began to get afraid.

That was when she thought about opening the door.

But she had never opened the door before, our friend who lived without a sky, and even the thought of that was enough to send her back to her chair, and hide her head in her hands. By now she felt like there was a wild beast loose inside her, clawing at her, and she knew that she would not be able to ignore it any longer, so she stood up, and walked across the room, and opened her door.

Outside was a corridor, and directly across the corridor was another door. That door was closed. She stood on her doorstep, our friend who lived without a sky, and she looked one way along the corridor, and then the other, and all there was as far as she could see were lines and lines of doors. None of them were opened.

She put one foot forward. Then the other. And at last she was standing outside. And she reached over, and she knocked on the door opposite.

Well, that knock sounded like the noise the world will make when it starts to break apart at the end of time. But it soon sank into silence. So she knocked again, and then a third time, and when this knock had sunk into silence, she was about to give up and go back inside her room, when she heard a *creeeeeeeeak...*

All around her, doors were opening. And from behind the doors, faces appeared, peering out. And some of these faces looked sleepy, and some of them looked angry, but most of them looked frightened. And when they saw each other, all of a sudden a babble of voices started up: *What is happening? Why isn't anything working? Do you know what's going on?* And most of all: *I don't know what to do. I don't know what to do.*

At last, the voices came down to two. And one of these voices said, *I'm going back inside*, and the other voice said, *I'm going to look round*, and our friend who lived without a sky found herself saying this, and as she said it, her voice grew louder and stronger. And some of the people around her – most of them, it should be said – shook their heads and went back inside and closed their doors, but a few nodded when they heard what our friend was saying, and told her they would follow her.

And off they went.

They tried each door as they went past, and some people came with them, and some people shouted at them to go away, and they came to the very last door, and behind it was a flight of stairs, going up. They went up the stairs, and came out onto another corridor. And they walked down this corridor, knocking on the doors, and some people came with them, and some people shouted at them to go away, and they came to the very last door, and behind it was a flight of stairs, going up. And on they went, on and on, and some people came with them, and most people shouted at them to go away.

After about an hour or maybe it was a thousand years or maybe it was something in between, they came up a flight of stairs and the door opened out onto the roof of the building. And they looked out around their world, which had no sky, and they saw a thousand towers just like theirs, and a thousand towers behind them, and high, high above them was a great ceiling. As they watched, all these people, our friend among them, they heard a great *creeeeeeak*, and they realised that the ceiling was cracking open. And then, at last, for the very first time, they saw the sky, and it was dark.

How beautiful it was, the sky! And they laughed with joy at how beautiful it was, and how glad they were to have seen it, while behind them, the towers were crumbling, and above them the ceiling was cracking, wider and wider, and behind these cracks stood the stars, which looked down upon the end of the world without pity or passion, and did not lend a hand.

Do you like that story? I made that one up myself. I made it all up, all of it. I saw a factory-town on the flicker screen once and I thought what it might be like to live there. Do you like that story? It was one of the first I made up, back before I had anyone to tell 'em to.

Once upon a time I never had anyone to tell my stories.

Four

The last stages of our journey to the smoky mountain were made in haste, and with a cloud above us. Two 'birds had been tracking us for a couple of days, and we were concerned about what we would find when we got there. We were meant to rendezvous with another band from the southeast, but there had been no 'casts from them in almost a week. Kal, I think, thought they were finished. Seffy, meanwhile, wouldn't hear a word of it. I wonder, looking back on everything that happened, whether Seffy's optimism sometimes slid into fooling herself. But she never seemed to worry; and if she was worried at the end she did a bastard good job of not showing us. You know what? I'll tell you what. I think Seffish woke each morning and looked at the sun and simply thought how glad she was to be alive. Like each new day was an unexpected gift. Maybe when you were a dance-fighter like her that really was how each day seemed. A bonus. Some of this rubbed off on the people around her. But I think those of us who were ordinary were scared most of the time, and most of all those last few days. Which was when, of course, we needed Seffy the most, and she came into her own.

We're a while from that yet though, and first you'll get to see us happy.

At last we reached the approach to the mountain. The trucks stopped. We all looked around. Our allies weren't here, that was plain enough. There was some muttering around me; people wondering why we'd come all this way to what was, after all, not much more than a bastard big rock in the middle of nowhere, no matter how many fancy stories we and the masters cooked up about it. I kept my mouth shut, my ears open, and my eyes wide. So I saw Kal jump out of the truck where the 'caster was kept. There was news, I could see, so I moved towards Crith and Seffy to hear what was going on. I only caught a few words before Kal saw me and, with a jerk of her thumb and a mouthed *fuck off* sent me on my way. I'd heard enough. There were people coming, but not our people. Soldiers were coming, up the road behind us.

Well, there was only one way now, and that was up, up the mountain, and hope that we were under cover of darkness before they put in an appearance. We got the trucks a little way up, and then it was no use.

Time we didn't have to spare got spent hiding them, ripping down vines and foliage, trying to make these bunches of green look natural. The 'caster was carried up by two people, like one of the masters' holy relics, and we trod our way up behind it, winding our way up, up, up the smoky mountain. We left people with the few pistols that we had at various points as we headed up – our defence, if you can call it that. Quite what the plan was supposed to be, I wasn't sure. We were heading up the only road available to us, and an army was coming behind, so quite how we were meant to get back down again, I wasn't sure. There we were, at the smoky mountain, and our people weren't there, and the masters were coming, and what was supposed to be a refuge was turning out to be a trap.

I remember stopping, footsore, and looking back down, and seeing that long black line marching towards us. I was nearly sick where I stood. That army, pulled together from somewhere, coming with only one purpose in mind, to grind us back into the rock. I thought about my home – because it was my home, the only one I'd known – that little scullery back at the fighting-school, and with all my heart I wanted to be back there, safe and sound, not stuck in the middle of all this. Whatever it was – a riot that got out of hand, an insurgence, a rebellion – I knew that I was too small for it, and way way out of my depth, and that nobody cared about my smallness in the great scheme of things, and there would be no pity for any of us, not even me, as inconsequential as I was, no mercy. As for the others – well, the masters are inventive, after all.

I am ashamed to say that at this point I started to cry or, at least, to sob. Thick, shuddering sobs. Pure despair. Oh, I was ashamed, so ashamed. I bit my lower lip, hard. That stopped the tears. I pinched my arm too, cutting off the sobbing. I rubbed my hand across my face, turning my back to the people walking behind me, my head down. Next thing I knew, Kal was there, like she always was, now I come to think about it. She stood next to me, and together we watched that line snake towards us. Then she spat on the ground.

Fuck 'em," she said, and she grabbed my hand, and dragged me on up.

After a while, we ran out of mountain. It got too steep, too narrow. Eventually, there was no safe path onwards, only a sheer drop. So we stopped, stopped still, and wondered what we should do next. The day was wearing on, the sun slipping down the sky. Below, the masters' army was making camp.

"Look at 'em," said Kal. "They're not fighters. They've pulled them off the fields and marched them here. They're scrapings, at best."

"Whatever they are," muttered Crith, "they'll enjoy killing us."

Seff smiled. "We'll take a fair few of 'em with us first."

"Yep," said Crith, "and there'll always be more where they came from."

The afternoon wore on. We watched the camp sprout up, like a fungus. We kept on at the 'caster, hoping to hear some news of our missing friends, hoping that they might come and save us. That was a dream. There wouldn't be enough, and they'd be fresh from a march. That lot down there would finish them. Besides, we didn't hear anything back. They were as good as disappeared into thin air, or sunk back into the rock. I think by this point we had all more or less given up. I was lying on my back, my head in shade under the long-hanging vines of a gnarled old tree, and trying not to think about anything. I don't remember much of that afternoon, but I do remember Seffy. She seemed to be everywhere, all at once, and when she was near you remembered you could smile.

And then somebody had a bright idea. One of the farm-hands, I should think. It wasn't the kind of idea that would come to the city people, I have to say, and I'm even prepared to admit that it was one of Oenith's lot that came up with the suggestion. Very smart it was too. The vines all over the mountain – they could be woven to make ropes. Yes, yes, they could, we did in on the plantation all the time. There are enough of us, we can make enough, let me show you how, yes, really, we did it all the time on the plantation...

Well, you can learn anything quick smart if you put your mind to it, and let's say that an army breathing up your arse makes you snap to attention pretty quick. Soon enough we were all hard at it, and I wonder if any of us have worked as hard as we did that afternoon and that evening, racing against the old sun as she lazed her way down the sky. You should have seen the state of our bastard hands – raggedy ruins, and still with ages to go. Even the fighters worked at it, and since we all knew that they had a hard night ahead the rest of us could hardly complain, and, besides, this was going to save our lives wasn't it? Funny how hard you can work when it matters. Funny how much you can slack when you're doing it for someone else. I've never worked that hard, not enough with Kal breathing down my neck.

Round about sunset, we realised that we were going to make it before the light died, and someone's voice lifted, and carried the rest of us with them. It's the song we all know, somehow, whoever we are and wherever we were born. Town or country, kitchen or farm or fighter, somehow we all know this. I heard us all, all of our sorry band, from Oenith's killers to my own dancers, singing our song, the song of the rock:

This is the rock, the rock of the world
The bones upon which everything rests
The channel for the water
The container for the soil
The surface for the air
The stuff that stars are made of
The first and the last
That lies behind the smoke upon the mountain
That lies beneath the streams and fields
The rock of the world is all is everything

I wonder sometimes how that must have sounded to the soldiers down at the foot of the mountain. Did they think that we were giving up? Did they think we were trying to raise our spirits before the end? Did they look at each other, and smile, and nod, and say, "Ah, well, they'll be dead in the morning." Or did they hear us all, singing like that, and realise who the dead ones were? Who the dead ones were.

Night fell. We looked down at the campfires. This was madness, wasn't it? It was a stupid idea. It would never work. But what did we have to lose? Down, down, on those woven ropes, went out fighters, the best of us, down the far side of the mountain. Soon enough we couldn't see them any longer, and all we could do was sit and wait as they crept their way round, and listen out until the killing started. That was our signal to come down and join in the attack.

Well, they weren't expecting us, and that gave us an advantage, but it wasn't one that was going to last long, if I'm honest, because those soldiers were mean, and, stars, they hated our guts. Some people – there's nothing they hate more than someone less well off than them. Makes them afraid, I think, that they could fall down that low. So they keep on kicking, as if to ward it off. As Kal said, Fuck 'em.

Still, you know, righteous fury can only get you so far, and, at the end of the day, there were more of them than there was of us. Once that initial shock of the ambush was over, they pulled themselves together, and they fought back like fucking beasts. I think I knew pretty quickly that there weren't enough of us. They started to push back; started to drive a wedge between us... I could see how it was going to end, the fighters cut off and surrounded, the rest of us pushed back up and picked off one-by-one.

And then – I don't know. It was like... It was like the rock of the world shook, suddenly, and seemed to move. Oh, but that can't happen, can it? The world doesn't shake and turn upside down. That's not how worlds work. But that was how it felt for a moment. We all stopped in our tracks, looked round, confused, frightened. And then I heard Seffy laugh; that golden laugh, and high, high, she lifted up her voice and she cried out:

"Where the fuck have you lot been?"

There were our friends, in the nick of time, relieving our fighters, and cutting off the soldiers from the road. We pushed back down from the mountain, pushed hard, and the fighters rallied, and our friends entered the fray.

What happened next? Well, you know, it was pretty bastard brutal. There weren't many of them standing by the time the old sun lifted its head again. But what did they expect? What, really, did they expect? It was only what we had expected, after all.

The Story of the Forked Logs

Here's another the masters like to tell. Can't think why. I'm going to tell it to you in their voice, because I can't tell a tale like this in my voice. It sticks in my throat and my tongue goes thick and the words won't come out. Some of our stories, they're shared, and the masters don't see how we're playing with them. And some of our stories are ours, and ours alone, and the masters have never heard them, and we'd cut out our tongues ourselves rather than tell them. But a story like this is theirs, and theirs alone, which I think probably makes it a lie.

Well, as you know, life can be a battle, and sometimes, with the hands, you start to think that on balance it might be quicker simply to do the job yourself. But that's not the way that the world was made, and one must honour the gods and the order of creation, or else things fall apart. Still, nevertheless, watching them sometimes as they blunder along can be a sore test, but that's only one of our burdens as masters. We are here to guide, and look after them, and they are here to serve, so that we can be free to think about how the world might be improved. It's a good arrangement, on the whole; it gets things done, even with occasional blunders.

Still, sometimes they need a little prompting, because, like children, they see the obvious rather than the most effective, which is a different category of thinking not always with their grasp. Here's an example. It's the story of the forked logs. You may have seen them about, here and there, and there are good reasons for that, which do not come into this story, but perhaps you don't know how they came about. The fact is that they came about out of frustration. Sometimes the hands seem almost to be wilful in their stupidity, and that was the case in the hand in this story.

As you know, it is the master's responsibility to learn the disposition and temperament of each of the hands which the gods have seen fit to provide. Some show an aptitude for a craft; a good master will encourage this, and the gods will show their approval through the bounty which accrues as a result. (A wise master, in these cases, will even go so far as to ask these hands the best way to go about a task. Sometimes, it might be surprise you to learn, the answers are sound, and the advice can be acted upon. I have noticed in these situations that the hand concerned returns to their work happier, glad, perhaps, to have had their suggestions acted on. As long as everyone is clear with whom the decisions lie.) Others, alas, are slower, heavy as the rocks and the stones with which they often show such odd affinity. One is inevitably burdened at some point with such as these, and must therefore find suitable tasks for them, within their abilities, which keep them busy. A hand with insufficient to fill the days often becomes unhappy and fractious, which naturally serves nobody. Keep them busy; there is enough time at the end of the day for rest, and a hand with plenty to do is serving the purpose of the gods and the order of things.

Yes, yes, back to the story. The forked logs. The hands in this story were not amongst the cleverest that had ever walked and worked, and one day was set the task of shifting a large number of stones from one end of the homestead to the other, in order to build a wall. At first light, the master gave them their instructions, and then left them to get on with it. Around the middle of the day, the master looked out to see how the work was coming along, and was horrified to see how little had been moved, barely a scratch on what needed to be done. So the master hung back, to see what method was being used, and was horrified to see that the hands were taking each stone one-by-one, rather than carrying them in bulk. Well, no wonder hardly any progress had been made! Well, the master had no time for such nonsense, and calling the hands together, gave them new orders, and watched as they piled the stones into sacks. Then they sent to find branches from the nearby copse within the master's lands, some long and some short, and they tied the shorter branch crossways at the top of the long pole, and from this they tied the sacks of stones. And at last they were able to carry more upon the backs.

Soon the work was underway, and proceeding at a much better pace, and the master watched for a while, marvelling at how such a simple solution had not occurred to the hands, and wondering how anyone ever got anything done. And the master was satisfied that the work would be done before nightfall, and so it was, which was better for the hands too because they would not have eaten until the work was done, even if that had meant waiting until dawn.

That's how the forked logs came about. They are the burden that the hands must carry, but as a result they do, on the whole, get the job done more quickly, which serves everyone's purposes, and above all, honours the gods and the order of creation.

I am sure we all have tales like this. As I say, sometimes they seem almost to be wilful in their stupidity.

Five

From what I've seen, people get a taste for killing. The first time – that's the test, and once you're past that, it becomes easier. I've never killed anyone, but I've seen a lot of killing. I don't know. I've never taken the plunge. I think I knew what I'd become.

We buried our people and left the rest for the birds. Then we left the smoky mountain, and struck north, heading towards the biggest of the east-west canals down here. There were a lot of us now – our troupe from Capallaire, plus our hangers-on, plus the people we'd picked up along the way, plus Oenith and her gang, and now the troupe that had come to our rescue. I'd say we were well onto a thousand by now. We had survived the first test, and winter was coming, and we needed a place to hole up and build up our strength and our reserves. I knew from listening (and because I could usually wheedle it out of Kal) that another big band was heading south, and we were going to meet them at the Big Lock.

It's not easy moving a thousand people. It takes a while, and it takes resources. The land around us had been worked hard for a long time, and we were out of season. Those were a hard days, struggling on, but at last we saw a subtle change in the land around us. We saw streams, and green. We were coming to lands where the masters wanted to live. And then, before we knew it, we were in the grounds of the house.

Oh, but it was beautiful! Can you imagine those gardens? I had never seen anything like them, not even at the flicks, where, besides, the colours are all faded. This was a real garden, maintained and cared for, with its own small canal running through. A big lawn stood before it – the most green I have ever seen – and Kal said to me that if we'd come here in the summer all the flowers would have been in bloom, and what did I think of that? I tried to picture that – the bright colours, yellow, red, pink, and purple – but I'm not sure my imagination did it credit. Sometimes you can only work with what you've got. Still, I did my best, and oh stars in my head it was ravishing, even out of season, and with the limits of my mind's eye.

Then we saw the wooden fork, and the body strung up on it.

I don't know if she was still living by then. Certainly she was dead by the time we got her on the ground. I slipped my way through to the front, but Kal saw me before I could get a good look and dragged me off... Besides, how do you think someone looks when they've been hanging up there in the hot sun for a while?

"Stay there," she said.

"Why?"

"There might be trouble," she said.

"What trouble?"

"For once, Iss, shut your trap and stay where I put you."

Well, it didn't take too long to work out what the trouble was, because I heard the voices raised in anger, and then I heard Oenith's voice, over everything else, and she was shouting about *Revenge*...

Some of us were trying to stop her; some of us were with her. The rest stood back to see where it would all fall. There weren't enough to hold Oenith and her people back. They ran towards the house, and it wasn't long before the family, who were hiding inside were dragged out onto that beautiful lawn. Some of their hands were trying to defend them. I think there were nearly a dozen altogether. I remember thinking: *All this green and water for so few people.* There were a couple of kids, not little ones, thank the stars, on the cusp. Big enough. Seffish and a few of our troupe ran forwards – much too late. The knives flashed in the sunlight, the blood ran like water, and that was the end of that.

Seffy and Kal just about stopped them burning down the house, but not before they did a lot of damage. Out came all the fine furnishings, the weavings and the paintings and the curtains and the cushions and all that shit they fill their houses up with, and as the old sun set, they lit the bonfire, and danced around it.

We kept to our side; Oenith's lot kept to theirs. I saw Kal, eyes glittering, watching them through the flames. Crith was at ease, and Seffish wanted to be, but was aware of Kal, tense beside her.

"Hey," Seffish said at last. "What's the matter?"

"Killing them was a mistake."

"It's done," said Seff. "It wasn't pretty, but it's done."

"It was the wrong thing to do."

"Is that pity?" said Crith. "After how they treated their hands?"

"Pity is for everyone," said Kal, although I'd like to say at this point that I hadn't seen much of this principle in action from old Kal over the years. "And, besides, it gives the masters an excuse to call us brutal. To use brutal means against us."

"They already do," said Crith.

Kal had to concede that. "But it doesn't help our cause," she said. "We go about like this, we'll never get the poor free on our side."

I saw Crith and Seffish exchange a look. Crith was puzzled; Seffish shrugged.

"Do we want them on our side?" said Crith.

"Yes," said Kal, at once.

"Why? What are they to us?"

"Nothing," said Kal.

"Well then," said Crith. She had one of Seff's hand clasped within her.

"Nothing yet. But we won't win without them. The masters need them. They need them to fight us. So we take them with us."

Crith laughed. "You're dreaming. They'll never side with us."

"They will when they work out that the masters only want them to do the fighting. To stand between them and us."

"They think we're shit. They think we're rubbish."

"Well," said Kal. "They'll soon see that we're not." She eyed Seffish. "What do you think, Seffy?"

Seff retrieved her hand from Crith's care. She stood, tall and strong and golden, and stretched out: her legs apart, her arms raised up to the heavens. If I had to believe in a goddess, I'd believe in her. Across the fire, Oenith was watching her too. Seff looked down at both Kal and Crith, and smiled, and said, "I think we should enjoy being alive."

The fire burned low. We slept, mostly. A few kept watch on the edge of our camp.

I woke in the dead of night. All around me I could hear the soft sounds of sleep, deep breathing, the odd sigh, someone twisting and turning. No nightmares; not tonight, not yet. I turned over to go back to sleep, but before I settled I heard someone moving around.

I kept to close to Seffy, I always did, and to Kal too. Old habits die hard. This dark shape, moving quickly and quietly through the night, was heading towards our leader. My first thought, oddly enough, was that Oenith had sent someone to murder her. Perhaps that explains why I opened my mouth and screamed.

Well, yes, obviously the whole camp was awake and on the move in no time. Seffy on her feet, Crith moments behind, and both bearing down on the would-be assassin. Except it wasn't some soft-footed killer from Oenith, or from anyone. It was a kid, almost as scrawny as me, but a lot more miserable-looking. Seeing the double strength of Seffish and Crith bearing down upon her, she crouched down on the ground, arms pulled over her head to shield herself. "Please!" she cried. "Please don't hurt me!"

Her name was Por, and she was from the house. They'd missed her when they pulled the family out. She'd hidden herself away in a quiet corner – we're good at that – but as the day wore on she realised we weren't going, and when night fell she decided to creep past us. But she was hungry, and the smell from our cooking fires pulled her our way. It was bad luck she'd headed straight for Seffy, and then I'd screamed. She was scared (of course she was, Por was scared most of the time I knew her): scared of us, scared of her masters, and scared that she'd be punished because they were dead and she wasn't. She kept coming back to this. It was an old law, after all. She should have put herself between us and them.

Meanwhile, at the far end of the camp, Oenith and her gang were ready to finish what they'd started. Not even Crith was ready for that, though. She and Kal and Seffy held a quick quiet conference, and then Por was given something to eat, and shoved into one of the trucks with a couple of our troupe outside.

Everything seemed settled for the night, and I was bedding down again when Kal came to find me. "Well," she said, "you got everyone's attention."

"Sorry," I said. "I was..."

"What, Iss? What were you?"

"I was scared for Seffy."

She looked at me thoughtfully. I wasn't afraid so much these days, I realised, that she was going to belt me. "Well," she said at last, "everything turned out all right, didn't it?"

"Sorry I gave you all a scare."

"You did the right thing."

Now that caught me on the hop. "Did I?"

A glimmer of a smile. "You called for help. You didn't go wading in yourself."

"Oh," I said.

"Go back to sleep," she said. "I'll get my own back in the morning."

That was how I got lumbered with baby-sitting Por.

Stars, she was a pain in the neck, and she didn't half cramp my style – as Kal intended, no doubt. Everywhere I went, she was bobbing around behind me. I'd be watching the dancers train, and she'd be hanging around. I'd go for a sniff about for news, and she'd be clacking away at my elbow. I think Kal had told her I'd look after her. Well, it put paid to a lot of my eavesdropping. "You're keeping out of mischief, Iss," Kal remarked one morning, and I thought, *Bastard cheek.* No chance of seeing or hearing anything with Por on my back, and she was too bastard good at sticking to me. I think she'd had her instructions too, straight from Seff, and she was in awe of Seffish, like everyone with any sense.

Well, eventually I gave up trying to lose her and resigned myself to having a shadow. I even started talking to her. Not that she said much. I mean, I know I can talk, or at least that's what Kal always said, but I do pause for breath occasionally, and sometimes I even ask direct questions, but Por would just stare back at me, her eyes wide open. Hopeless. Then, late one afternoon (we were back on the road by then, trudging along), she said, "What do we do when the soldiers come?"

I didn't know she'd spoken at first; I wasn't used to hearing a voice come from that direction. She asked me again.

"Eh?" I said. "What soldiers?"

Well, I'd only missed out on the big news of the day, which is that the masters had five hundred heading our way, trying to stop us get to the Big Lock. We were on the march right now to get us to safety so that the fighters could turn round and face them. I don't know which made me angrier: that I'd missed out on news, or that bastard Por had heard it first. I was still seething when we made camp. Then the fighters went off, and we sat down to wait. Kal got us all working, mending clothes, fixing tools, getting food ready, keeping us busy. Por came and sat down beside me, hunched over in a crouch, watching me build a fire.

"Iss," she said, after a while. "I got a question."

"Oh yeah? What?"

"Who are my masters now?"

I had to check she wasn't mucking around with me. "Eh? What do you mean?"

"Who are my masters now?"

No, she wasn't joking. "Well, nobody."

"Nobody?"

"Yeah," I said. "Or you're your own master. That's the point."

Por didn't answer right away. And then I realised she was crying, all soft like, and trying to hide it from me, as it if was something to be ashamed of, or perhaps because she thought it would mean trouble.

"Hey," I said, putting a hand on her arm. "It's all right. It'll be all right."

After a while the crying stopped, and she sniffed and wiped her arm across her face. She looked at me, and I thought she'd be happy, maybe, but she wasn't. She was scared. She was scared out of her wits. Por was always, always scared. That's what life had done to her.

We won, of course. The first messengers came back a little before sunset, and soon the whole camp knew. About an hour later, the fighters returned. Most of them. There was Oenith, looking miserable, and last of all came Seffy and Crith, looking like queens.

I heard later that Oenith had wanted to concentrate all our forces, but that Seffy and Crith had insisted on coming at the army from two directions, and that was what had won the day. Two enemies vanquished. Seffish was our undisputed leader now, with Crith by her side. We welcomed them amongst us – our beautiful dancers – and there, right in the middle of us, Seffy pulled Crith into her arms, and they kissed, and in the last of the sun they shone as if they were made of gold, hard-won, hard-worked gold. Then the sky went dark and the stars came up and there was such a party you wouldn't believe. I will never forget the dancers that night – dancing for the sheer joy of being alive in the world and free from trouble. The dance as it should be; not what it was made to me.

Looking back now I can see that was the best day. The day when we were most together. The day when anything was possible – when it seemed that even this sorry old story could only have a happy ending.

Part 2

WINTER

Six

Winter came, as it always does. After the battle, our way to the Big Lock was clear, so we marched down there and set up shop. There was a big party of us there already, and two or three arrived over the next few weeks, taking us to nearly ten thousand, I'd guess.

Seffy's reputation went before her. She was famous in her own right, of course, but the story of the escape from the smoky mountain, and then overwhelming the master's forces had made that reputation even stronger. She looked the part; she looked like a living statue that you'd raise to a hero from a story, or to one of the master's strange gods only real. Everyone knew her; everyone wanted their moment with her. Like a star from the flicks. She didn't change. Seffy never changed. There was always that strength and that grace, and that sense that she saw herself as no different from any of us. That, I think, as much as the physical beauty was what pulled people to Seffish; that sense she gave you that you mattered as much as anyone else, mattered for your very own self, not what use you were or what value you held. She loved you because you were... you. I don't think most of us had felt that before. Do I sound like another acolyte? It's hard not to be. (And let's not forget Crith, always beside her, watching all this adulation with more than a little amusement; and Kal, of course, just behind her, whispering advice.)

It's hard, with all these years between, to give you an impression of our town as it was that winter. The canals aren't as important these days, of course, not now the 'birds are everywhere, but in those days they were the veins of the land. They linked the big towns, and little side-canals went off, like branches on a tree, to join the smaller towns together. The one that passed through the Big Lock was the main route for traffic through the south.

I hear these days that people holiday on the canals. Back then, they were too busy, working routes, and I don't think anyone could find rest and recreation between the sacks of goods and the livestock. There's not as much water in them these days either, of course, and it takes longer to shift stuff about than using 'birds. I can't ever imagine holidaying on one. I look at those old things, and I see the work that went into them, the tons of rock and soil shifted, and the lives that must have been lost and still lie buried deep in the rock of the world. We lived there, worked; we didn't rest. We made a town there, a place to be. We built, we traded; we fixed and mended. And most of all we defended the land behind us, and watched the land ahead.

There was beauty there, though, I won't deny that, even in winter. At the day's end, sometimes, with the white cold sun on her way to her rest, I would walk down the tow-path, under the arc of bare trees. I tried to picture it in the summer, with the leaves full and green, shading you from the hot day as you walked along, the water sluggish beside you. I would not see summer by the Big Lock. I never have and I never will. Perhaps it's peaceful. Perhaps it's nice. Perhaps it's a good place to take a holiday.

The days passed, busily. From what information we could gather via the 'casters, we believed we were safe until the spring. The masters would not move on us till then. That was a strange place to be, a kind of limbo, safe for now but with that huge threat lying ahead. Winter wasn't kind, but nobody wanted it to end. It isn't right not to look forward to spring.

Our numbers continued to grow. All of our main groups had come in from the south now, so in that sense we were at full complement. What we hadn't expected was the appearance of free folk among our number. I say that – Kal had expected it, had hoped for it, as I've said; this united front, she thought, was the only way we were going to have any kind of lasting victory. I don't think she had expected them in this number, however.

They didn't come in big bands, not the way we did, a troupe of fighters protecting a larger party of old and young. They came in little groups, no more than half-a-dozen, one homestead at a time. Sometimes they brought their hands with them; sometimes their hands were long gone, had already slipped away to find us, leaving their free-folk behind. Imagine what those meetings must have been like! You have to laugh at the thought of that.

Where did they come from, I hear you asking. Haven't you been listening? The land for those big farms, the kind Oenith and her lot worked, it had to come from somewhere, you know. The masters, the rich ones, had taken what they could by law. Now they were taking the rest by force. Bigger was better all round, they said; more productive, more efficient. The only problem was that there were already people living there. Sometimes, if the land was good enough, and the owners sharp enough to see the way the wind was blowing, they'd sell. They'd take what was left and try their luck in the towns. But some people didn't want to sell. They liked their lands and their homesteads; they liked the way they'd been living all these long years -- generation after generation, some of them -- and they didn't see why they should move on. These were the ones that often ended up coming our way.

You could see from their faces they hadn't expected how ruthlessly the masters had dealt with them. Well, I didn't feel much pity for that, I admit. They could see, every day, how the masters worked, by looking at us, at the way we were handled. Some of them must have treated us that way themselves. Did they think it would never come their way? That being called free in name would make them that way for real? What a bunch of idiots. Still, they made a sorry sight on the whole, clutching the bits and pieces of their possessions to them, trying to cling on to what made them different from us.

I remember one afternoon, watching one particular group arrive. Por was with me, of course; Kal was too. Five of them. An old one, sitting on the back of a cart, pulled by the two strongest. Two younger ones walking beside. I heard Kal sigh.

"Problem, Kal?"

"Oh, there's always a problem," she said. "The trick is to turn it to your advantage." She nodded at the bigger of the young ones. "That one looks about your age. Why don't you two go over and make her welcome?"

"You telling us what to do again?"

"Yep," she said, and went on her way.

Well, we did go over and say hello, Por and I, but not because Kal told us to. No, really. The truth was I liked the look of the girl, and, besides, I thought, it wasn't going to do any harm. This was how I met Atellaire.

Turned out they were two separate parties. Tella – as we came to call her in time – had been travelling with the old woman. The other three – all hands – had met them on the road, and had kindly offered to help. Knowing Tella as I did later, that must have been some journey, as she tried to boss those hands around. I imagine that they soon became very good at not hearing what she was saying. I'm pretty sure, too, that Tella hadn't realised where they were heading until it was too late. Anyway, she helped the old woman down from the cart, there were some awkward farewells with the others, and then she and the old lady just stood there, looking round, trying to work out what was going on.

"Hey," I said. "Need some help?"

They looked at us with mistrust. I saw the old woman swallow – literally, swallow – her pride. "Please," she said. "We have nothing..."

"None of us have anything, really," I said. "What we've got we share."

Well, it was clear to me very quickly that there wasn't much left in the old woman. Por had seen it too. We each took an arm, helped her walk. Tella came behind.

"Where to?" said Por.

I thought about that. People like these two, free poor, wouldn't be welcome everywhere round here. But close to Kal they might get a little less trouble. So we took them to our part of the camp, where Seffish reigned supreme, and Kal through Seffish, and found some spare coverings for a tent, and helped them put it up, and then we found them water and something to eat. After that, the old woman slept. Por and I sat Tella down outside and asked her questions.

They were from further north, although still south of the capital, which was much gentler country than down here, and very desirable. Her family had a farm; theirs for generations. Then someone bought the land upstream from them, and then downstream, and soon they were surrounded...

Well, I could see where this story was heading, and I think Por could too. Tella, however, looked to me as if she still couldn't believe what had happened, even though it had happened to her. "It was dark," she said. "There'd been a few weeks of trouble – you know, fences damaged, livestock let out... I think they were trying to scare us off. But we'd farmed that land for ever. It was *ours*..."

Yes, well, sometimes being scared off is the right thing to do. That dark night, Tella woke coughing through thick smoke. The homestead was on fire. She got out. The rest of the family, six of them, didn't escape.

"At dawn it rained," she said. "Too late. I tried to go back inside..."

"Fuck, no," I said, and reached for her hand. She let me take it. Sometimes you take comfort where you can.

"There wasn't anything left –"

"Well, no," I said. "There wouldn't be." I looked worriedly at Por, who was twisting her hands around. "Hey," I said, "you should try to put all this out of your mind. It won't do you any good, going over and over it. Try not to think about it."

She looked at me as if I was mad. "How? How do I forget something like this?"

Well, I didn't know how to answer that. You saw horrors every day, didn't you, or thought about horrors you'd heard about, and you had to put them out of your mind otherwise you'd be done for. I looked at Por, who must have seen some pretty terrible things. "You just do," I said, lamely.

"Oh well," Tella said. "I suppose it's different for you."

Carefully, I let go of her hand. "Hey, Por," I said. "We should let Tella get some sleep."

"It's still early," said Por, useless as ever.

"Yeah," I said. "She should get some sleep anyway."

I would've kept my distance after that, but it turned out that if I wanted to find Por, I had to look first for Tella. Yes, I know what I said: Por was a pain in the neck. But she was company. I'd got used to her being around. And now she wasn't around.

Well, I found her, hurrying across the camp with a couple of jugs of water.

"Hey," I said. "Where you going?"

"Tella needed some help," she said. Gave me a guilty look. *Oh yes, Mistress Tella*, I thought, *I'm onto you.*

I took one of the jugs off her. "Yeah?"

"The old woman isn't too well."

The old woman, last I'd seen, had been sitting up outside her tent watching the world go by with a jaundiced eye, muttering jaundiced thoughts about all she could see. "Oh yeah?"

"Just trying to help, Iss."

We reached Tella's tent. I hung back to see what happened. Tella came out, clocked that Por only had one jug, and said, "Where's the other one? I said two!" Then she saw me.

I slung the other jug round and dumped it on the ground at her feet. I said, "What you say when someone lugs your water over for you, is thank you."

"Leave it, Iss," Por said, unexpectedly. "It's all right. I was only helping."

Helping. Tella was making herself busy with the water now, but the old woman was watching me, and she had this little smile on her lips that made me want to wallop her.

"Helping," I said. "All right. You keep on helping. I'll see you later."

I went off, yes, all right, in a huff, I'll admit, and when I looked back over my shoulder, I could see Por was making a fire for them, getting their supper going. I bet they didn't offer her anything, or only the scrapings. More fool her. I swore I wouldn't go near them again, that Por was welcome to her new masters, but in fact I was drawn back again and again. Not because Kal had asked me to, no. The problem, you see, was Tella. The problem was that I had never in my life seen anyone as beautiful as her

Late that night I heard, rather than saw, one of the masters' 'birds circling, circling overheard.

The Story of the Hand Who Got There Second

Once upon a time there was a hand who loved to work in wood. From a young age, this hand could be found chipping away at the firewood, trying to make shapes and so on. Well, this is the kind of thing that a clever master doesn't miss, so as soon as the hand was anywhere near big enough, her master apprenticed her to a carpenter, one of the free folk who lived nearby. They struck a nice bargain: the master paid a sum for the time it would take to do the teaching, and, once the hand was good enough, the carpenter would keep the hand for a year and a day, and take half of whatever the hand earned while the master took the rest.

Now, this hand was a very quick study, and the carpenter, who loved her craft, took to her new apprentice and grew fond of her. The carpenter, you see, had no family of her own, and had often thought how good it would be to have someone who would want to learn all that she knew. And in fact perhaps a child of hers would not have wanted to know how to work in wood, while the hand was very keen, so everyone in this case was happy. It wasn't long before the carpenter brought the hand into her house – her very own house! – and even built a bed for her there, rather than in the workshop. They were like a family.

Everything went along very well. The hand learned the trade much quicker than anyone had expected, and the carpenter went back to her master and said, "Now, about our bargain. Your hand is ready to work by herself now, and according to our terms she should come back to you. But listen to me. I can teach her even more, teach her how to do fine work, and I promise you she will learn to earn you even more. So let her stay with me a while longer, and learn everything I know, and you will take half, and I will take half, and everyone will be happy."

The truth was, of course, that the carpenter didn't want the hand to go, because she was used to her company, and didn't want to be alone, but this is no argument as far as the masters were concerned, which is why she said what she did. But the hand's master saw that this plan made good sense, and agreed to it. And so began a good and productive time, when the carpenter and the hand worked happily together, and the workshop was always busy, and the hand learned new skills and produced finer work, as good as a master crafter if the truth be told. The carpenter was delighted with the hand's progress, and could see that she could be even better with the right information. So, secretly, she taught the hand to read.

Well as you know, the masters, as a rule, don't like us knowing what the marks on pages mean, and free-folk can find themselves in trouble for this kind of thing. So they kept this secret between them, and it made them greater friends than ever, and it made the hand even better at her craft, since she could now measure properly, and work with numbers, and everyone was amazed at how good her work was, and said what a fine teacher and crafter the carpenter must be to be able to get such work out of a hand. And their fame grew around that part of the country, and soon enough business was booming and everyone was happy.

One evening, when the work was done and the hand had finished clearing away the supper, she said that she wanted to show the carpenter something that she had been working on now for some time, if the carpenter was willing. And the carpenter *was* willing, and most interested to see her apprentice's work. But the hand didn't bring out a piece of wood – she brought out from her pocket a little notebook, lovingly made, the bindings hand-sewn. Quite where she had found the paper, the carpenter didn't know, as there wasn't so much about the workshop, and the pencil, too, was a question unresolved. Still, the carpenter put these matters aside and started to look through the notebook.

Inside were all sorts of drawings, lines and triangles and circles, and handwritten notes laboriously made. And, shyly, the hand said that she had, over the years, begun to notice all kinds of relationships between these, and started to jot them down, and she wondered what her friend thought of that. Well, the carpenter, looking closely, soon understood what the hand had been doing, and when she did she burst out laughing.

"Why," she said, "this isn't new! We've known all this for hundreds of years!"

The hand nodded, and took back the book, and put it in her pocket. And while she kept on using her books, she never mentioned them to the carpenter again. At the end of the year, her master came to see how business had been, and whether the contract was still going well, and if the hand should come back to her estate. And the hand said that she would go back to her, and said goodbye to the carpenter on friendly terms. The carpenter was sad to see her go, and missed her for a long time, and all she had earned with her, but soon took another apprentice, the child of a neighbour, who was eager to learn, if not as quick. And that was the end of that.

Here's a thing about this story. Some people think it's funny. Some people think it's the saddest thing they've ever heard. What do you think it is?

Seven

So there we were, the three of us, sort of stuck with each other really. I mean, it was a big camp by then, but I'd got used to having Por around, but now you could only find Por around wherever Tella was. This is the thing about the masters, you see. They have this poise, this ease. It makes you feel oh so small. It makes you feel like you were born to do what they said. Nobody in Tella's life had ever told her she was worthless. That she couldn't expect better. But, I mean, what was she, after all? A farmer's kid. Mucking about with livestock and in the dirt or whatever it was they did on those blasted homesteads of theirs. She even said, one morning, that she had never been to a city, or not even a town, not even one as small as Capallaire. Well, that gave me a laugh. All her bossiness and big talk, and she had never seen much past those fields of hers.

"Never?" I said, with as much scorn as I could muster. I spun a fine story then, a story about Capallaire, its life and its busyness; the smells and the noise and the dirt; the tears and the laughter. Conjured up a few characters that I had known and loved, and only put a little spin on them, but that's allowed in stories, isn't it? A bit of garnish. As I talked, I could see Por's eyes opening wider and wider, and when I started on my stories of the people she laughed out loud. Is there anything better than working your craft with a story? Seeing that you're carrying someone with you? Makes you feel clever. Makes you feel loved, like you can work a special magic, if there was such a thing in this old hard world.

"I bet, Por," I said, knowing full well what the answer would be, "that you've not seen the flicks, either."

Por shook her head, wordless.

"What about you, Tella?"

She was building a fire. She wasn't completely hopeless, I'll give her that.

"Of course not," she said. "We lived way out."

Well, then I couldn't resist it. I loved the flicks, you might have worked that out by now; I would have spent all my time there if I could have got away with it, and I knew the best houses in the town, and I knew the way to get into the pit without having to pay, either sneaking in the side door or doing favours for someone there... Oh, those stories!

Those pictures, shimmering! Once I got started I couldn't stop myself. I went on and on about how much I looked forward to it, my schemes for getting in when I didn't have a piece or a bead to my name, the characters who owned or worked the places – yes, at least as good as what you saw on the screens, some of them. The creepy old woman at the big hall near the centre with no teeth and bad breath who always gave me a sweet which I didn't really want from her, or the door-hand at the poky little hall up the hill who would never let me in and was mad as a beast to see me in the pit...

And all this was before we'd even started, before we'd got to the main event! The hall would go dark, later than planned, usually, and everyone sitting on the floor around you went *Oooooooo!* which was a joke, of course, because we'd seen all this before, but wasn't a joke, of course, because we were here because we wanted to be transported. Well, and then the screen flickered, and you cheered, and (with a stop and a start most usually) the pictures started running. And each time was different – you cried at the love stories or you gasped at the pictures of strange stars and the strange worlds or you cheered the dancers, cheered them as they fought, cheered for Seff or Crith, whichever way you leaned. And what was best (although I didn't say this then, I was completely daft) was how safe you felt, in that hall, with all those other people, sitting there on the floor together, being happy and not worried about anything, and altogether sharing that feeling of being that way... Oh, I could talk about the flicks forever!

"Well," said Tella, turning back to tend the fire. "I'm sure you must have enjoyed it."

And that was that. With that, it all became wrong, somehow. Gaudy and cheap and sentimental, the sort of thing that the worst kind of person would like. The kind of person who wasn't good for anything much, really. I went dead quiet.

And then Por said, "I think it sounds nice, Iss."

Oh stars, that was the worst of the whole bastard thing! Because Por had seen Tella cut me down, and she felt sorry for me. Oh, that was deepest cut! I stood up, burning, burning, my fists clenched tight together and what felt like the rock of the world itself stuck at the back of my throat, and I said, "Oh, fuck you, Por! Fuck you!"

Then I kicked Tella's fire over and went on my way.

Well, nothing went unnoticed in our part of the camp, and so I guess word of this got back to Kal in next to no time, if she hadn't been watching already. But it was Crith, strangely enough, who had something to say about the whole business, coming to loom over me as I thumped away at Kal's washing. (Yes, sometimes I still did that as a favour for her, because she was so busy doing so many other things, which I think is fair enough. But these days she always asked, and that's what made the difference.)

Well, I know that this story has been mostly about Seffish and Kal so far, because I was in love with Seffy like pretty much all of us, and Kal – well, Kal was Kal and one of life's bastard constants. So I know I've not talked much about Crith, but don't make the mistake of writing her off. Crith is just as important in this story. Seffy was nothing, not really, without Crith. She was a check, a balance, the one who stopped Seffy was soaring too high above us. Between them, those three – Seff, and Crith, and Kal – should have conquered the whole world. Except they didn't, and there we are.

Well, there I was, in quite the temper, and I saw Crith and I scowled, guessing I was in for some kind of trouble, for something or other, because Crith didn't make herself felt very often, and I was usually in trouble for. But she wasn't shouting, and her hands weren't lifted, so I sat back on my heels and waited for the reckoning.

"Hey," she said.

"Hey."

"You doing that for Kal?"

"Yeah."

"Do you take in other people's washing?"

I glared at her. "You laughing at me?"

"Me laugh at you? Why would I do that? And what would you do about it if I was?"

"I'd dunk your bastard head in this filthy water."

"Like to see you try, Iss. That'd give me the laugh I wanted."

I carried on wringing the clothes, like I was wringing someone's neck *naming no names*, and then I checked the water, which wasn't too bad, all things considering, so I stored it in the container where I could use it again. When I turned round, Crith was hanging up the washing, which was nice of her, she didn't have to do that kind of thing for the little people. Which was what I was, after all. Little people.

"It's hard," she said, "not to be the loved one. But don't bend yourself out of shape for someone else, Iss. That's a mug's game." Then she looked at the container of water and said, "I'll bring my stuff over later. But if you use that mucky stuff on it I'll dunk *your* bastard head in it." And then she went on her way.

Well, I kept my distance after that. Tella and Por were busy – well, Por was – and I could certainly find plenty to do, or Kal could find me something if I couldn't. So I didn't see much of them over the next few weeks. I ran errands for Kal, all over the camp, and I did what I did best, and what I figured was what she really wanted from me, which was to slip in and out unnoticed, and hear everything that was going on.

There were a lot of us – a real big town, though not a town like the masters would think of it, with their stone buildings all stacked up one on top of the other. We had tents, a bit of salvaged wood from here and there, and the place was as scruffy as we were. And there were so many of us. Thousands and thousands, tens of thousands. Yes, I know, you're looking at me like I'm making up a story, exaggerating, but really – there were loads of us. Why hadn't we thought before how much strength we had, if we could only get together somehow? How had the masters managed to persuade us that we were nothing? We weren't nothing. We were legion. They must have been shitting themselves up in their big tall towers in the capital.

I'm not saying all was sweetness and light, no way! There were a lot of scarred and desperate people; some of them nasty bastards. They'd lived bad lives on the big farms, with no pity, nothing but hard work and hard knocks, the fear of pain driving them on, and they didn't just turn up to our town by the Big Lock and turn into smilers. There was anger, and a lot of fists, and two or three times that winter there was a killing. Did I feel safe, living in all this? What? Of course not. But I didn't feel safe living in Batiaire's kitchen, did I? I don't mean dodging a slap from Kal. There isn't safety, not for us, not anywhere. What if Batiaire had lost all her money all of a sudden, or decided to sell up and retire? We'd've been up on the market, in the click of someone's fingers, to settle the debts or pay for her retirement in the sunshine. Where would I have ended up then? I didn't have talents. I didn't have a skill at making or mending to give me some value. I had my body, that was all, and there were lots of bodies about. You can use bodies up fast, there's always more coming. So, yes, I was scared sometimes, because there were some bad people about. But the difference was that most of us understood that we had something in common, and that all the pain we each felt from this hard old world couldn't be allowed to wreck that.

Most of that winter we worked, well, like hands. Hard work feeding that many, and then we knew that with the spring the masters would be coming, and we had to prepare for that. Not a week went by when a 'bird didn't fly past, counting how many we were, how big we were getting. So we were making weapons too, in between everything else. Enough to keep everyone busy.

The free folk amongst us didn't like that. No, I'm not being fair. There were some who knew that their situation was desperate, and had understood that they were expendable. I have no complaint about that. But one or two... Well, they didn't like taking orders from hands. That was their job, they thought. And one or two of us, as I've already said, couldn't get out of the habit of taking orders.

Yes, well, I couldn't avoid Por and Tella for ever, could I, not least because I got the sense from Kal that she was keen for us to make it up. "Shouldn't be strife amongst us," she would say, pointedly, whenever Por ran past. So I wandered that way one day, to the little tent the three of them shared. And there was Tella, bossing Por about, and Por doing what she was told. I hung back until Por dashed off on some errand or other, and then marched up.

"Oh," said Tella. "It's you."

"Yes, it's me."

"How are you?"

"I'm fine," I said. "You look like you're thriving. How's Por."

"Por?" she shrugged. "Fine, I guess."

"Still bossing her about?"

Tella sighed. "Oh do stop. Por doesn't mind."

"How do you know?"

"I know."

"If she doesn't mind," I said, "it's because she doesn't know better."

"Why would she know better?" Tella said. "It's what hands are for, isn't it?"

I remembered Kal saying she didn't want strife and I didn't belt her. Instead I said, "Are you blind? Are you stupid?"

She didn't answer right away. After a moment she said, in a very low voice, "You're not to talk to me like that."

"No? Why not?"

"Because you're just —"

"Go on," I said. "Say it."

But she didn't, or not straight out. "These things," she said, "fetching and carrying — they're not my job! Por is used to it. She's happy doing it —"

"Don't you get it?" I shot back. "The work's shared now. If you're going to keep on living here, Tella, you've got to understand that."

She shook her head. "I'm not staying here. I'm going home as soon as I can."

"Home? What home? Not your farm. That's carved up now. They didn't care about you. You were in the way. This," I said, looking round at the mess and the madness and the hope and the work, "this can be your home." I don't think she would have heard me pleading.

"No it can't."

"So where, Tella? One of the cities? What will you do there?"

"You know, I'm not afraid of hard work —"

"Yes, there's work in the cities, but do you know what kind? Factories. Fucking. Is that what you want?"

Well, this whole conversation wasn't going anywhere, was it, so after a few more frosty bites and fiery hits from me I stamped off and left her to it. Not much later, Por appeared by my elbow.

"Hello," I said. "Had enough of her?"

"Shut up," she said.

Well, that caught me the hop. "You what?"

"Shut *up*, Iss. Keep out. Mind your own bastard business. Is that clear enough?" She started to go.

"Hang on!" I scrambled to my feet and went after her. I put my hand on her, friendly, nothing meant by it, and she shook it off.

"You shouldn't say things like that! She was upset!"

"*She* was upset —"

"She lost everyone, Iss!" Por said. "Everyone she loved died!"

"There's that old woman —"

Por gave a sour laugh. "Her? She's a hard-faced old beast. Tella met her on the road, wouldn't leave her. Everyone died, Iss. All her family."

Well, I felt bad about that. At least all my dancers were safe. And Kal, of course.

"I'm helping because I want to," Por said. "You've got to get that into your thick head. Because I want to."

She went off. I thought about what she'd said, and how she'd said it. And I'd never heard Por talk like that before. So, later, I went looking for Tella. I hung around until Por was out of the way, then went up to her.

"Oh," she said. "You again."

"Don't start. I'm here to say sorry."

She looked up at me, suspicious, like she was searching my face for the truth. "Sit down," she said.

"Don't boss me," I said.

"Please," she said, patting the ground, "won't you sit down?"

"That's more like it."

She found some drinking water for both of us, which was a nice gesture. We eyed each other over the rims of the cups. "I thought about what you said," she said.

"Er, which bit?"

"About the work being shared. I'm not lazy, you know. On our farm we only had one hand, and she was getting old to be honest. I did more than my fair share!" Her face crumpled suddenly. "Affy, her name was. She looked after me when I was small. She used to sing a song, a song about the rock of the world..."

Stars, she was beautiful, and she looked so sad and lost. I said, softly, "You can make a home here, you know. A real home. You can help us, and learn from us. But you can't expect us to serve you. That's not how it works any more. It's not how it should work, not anywhere."

"I know," she said. "I do get it."

"Por," I said. "Nobody's ever been kind to her. Her whole life. A tiny bit of kindness, and she'll be yours for life. But that's not fair on her. She shouldn't be anyone's."

"It's good," she said, "how you look out for her."

"I'm just trying to make this all work."

We sat and drank from our cups. After a while, Tella said, "What about you, Iss?"

"What about me?"

"Has anyone ever been kind to you?"

I had to think about that. Not Kal, that wasn't the deal. Seffish? Crith? They looked out for me, and I know I made them laugh, but kind? "Don't worry about me," I said. "I get by. I always get by."

The Story of the World Turned Upside Down

Well, here's a story, one you'll think you've heard before, but you won't have, because it's a story that I made up apart from the bits that you've heard before.

As you know, there is only one thing in this old world that brings the masters and the hands together, and that's the festival of the shortest day, the day the world turns upside down. Well, I know that you know all about that festival, and what fun it can be when everyone does it right. The masters and the hands swap round, and the masters serve the hands for the day. I am sure too that you know the story of how this festival came about, but let's have it anyway, or something close.

"Oh," said Tella, "I love this story. We told it every year the night before the festival."

"I love it too," said Por. "We told it too the night before. It makes me feel safe."

Oh dear, I thought, they're not half going to be cross with me... But I went on told it my way anyway.

Well, we hands have our own ideas about where this festival comes from, but I won't bother you with that for now, because either you know it already or else you don't really care what hands tell each other, given as we're largely known to be tale-tellers and story-spinners of the highest order and that's yet another reason that we can't be trusted. So let's hear the masters' version of events, because it is a very pretty story, and it makes them seem ever so nice. The masters, who believe in this kind of thing, say that back at the start of history, their strange old gods…

"I wish you didn't say that," said Tella.

"Said what?" I said.

"Said 'strange old gods'. They're not strange. They're the gods."

"They're your gods, Tella," said Por.

"Shall I tell this story or are you to going to keep on yapping all night?"

"Tell the story, please, Iss."

The masters, who believe in this kind of thing, say that back at the start of history, their bastard old gods used to visit the world sometimes, in disguise, and walk around amongst people, to make sure that things were ordered the way they were supposed to be. And sometimes they'd jog our elbows, or nudge us in the right direction, and remind a hand about what she was meant to be doing, and encourage a master to think harder and deeper and better. And one night, the night before the day when the world turns upside down, the sky-god and the water-god decided to come and have a look round, and see how things were done. Well, everyone was busy and rushing about, and didn't have much time for two old strangers wandering around, and very soon the day was wearing on, but no matter who they stopped and asked, they couldn't find a bed to sleep upon that night.

Well, at the edge of the town was a humble old house, where an old woman lived with her hand. Between them they had next to nothing, and the hand had least of all, and on top of everything else that old woman was blind, couldn't see her fingers in front of her face, and if the gods came knocking at the door, she couldn't have recognised them. As for the hand, as you know, hands don't care for the old gods much, so she wouldn't have known what to look for, and, besides, she was out on an errand anyway.

Well, the two gods came at last to this old house, and they looked at each other, and they looked at the weather, and they thought: *Nothing ventured,* and they knocked on the door. That old woman wasn't sure what to do at first. Her hand was out, and wouldn't be back for a while, and she never had visitors, and so she called through the door to ask who was there. "Two strangers," said the sky-god, "looking for a bed on a cold old night."

Well, anyone with any sense would know not to open their door to strangers on a dark night, but this old woman had a soft heart, and so she opened the door, and she did not recognise the gods, of course, but she welcomed the strangers into her house. And they sat, and tried to make themselves warm although there wasn't much of a fire, and she gave them a bite, although there was nothing to spare, and then they sat and told tales and sang songs, and altogether had a fine old time, and at last the old woman fell asleep.

"Oh," said Tella, "here is the bit I love most."

"It's nice this bit," said Por.

And I shouldn't have done it, I know, but sometimes I can't help myself.

Well, the gods made themselves comfortable by the fire, and on the whole they decided they were not displeased with how their evening was gone, and they were glad to find that in the world there was still some kindliness, and how it was always in the places where you didn't expect it, wasn't it, and they said to each other what a poor house this was, and that something should be done. And then they lay down and went to sleep.

Not long after this, the hand came back.

"Hang on," said Por. "That's not right."

"No, no, no," said Tella. "The hand doesn't come home till morning. She stopped for a drink with an old friend and fell asleep and when she gets back the house is full of food and there's a big fire in the hearth and the gods are gone —"

"Hey," I said, *"this is my story and I'll tell it my way."*

Not long after this, the hand came back. She had walked halfway across town and then back again to find some fuel for the fire, and she was cold and she was wet and above all she was fed up. Well, she took one look at those two strangers, asleep by the fire, and she thought, "That bastard old witch, she'll have given them my supper and she'll have me waiting hand and foot on them tomorrow if I know her."

So, quick as a flash, she picked up the strangers' coats, and she felt inside the pockets. And in one pocket she found a bag of pieces, and in the other pocket, she found some precious stones, and she thought, "I can do something with these." So off she went, with her own pockets full now, and she had a good time spending it. When she came back to the house, carrying her bargains, the strangers had gone, and she set up the house with food and fire. And the rest of the pieces and the stones she tucked away for a rainy day, because after all her master was old, and not long for this world if the truth be told. That's the end of that.

I told this one to Por and Tella one night, the night before the festival, and, oh my, what a quarrel we had about it! Who would have thought a daft old story could cause so much strife. But there it is: stories can be funny like that, and if people don't get what they're expecting, they can get ever so cross. Well, Por laughed and laughed and laughed and said I shouldn't be allowed to muck about with a good old tale like that, and I said who's stopping me eh? And she laughed and laughed and laughed again and said that was fair enough. But Tella! Oh how mad the story made her, really mad, so that was job done.

Eight

Midwinter came, and with it the big festival, the one that everyone shared, free or hand. The day of the year when the world turned upside down. Well, I've heard that in those fancy country houses this is a real celebration, huge, lasting days, with plenty of visitors and lots and lots of food and drink. But the highlight was always the shortest day, when the hands and the masters swapped jobs, and the hands sat down at the table and the masters waited on them. Well, that's a big joke, isn't it? Like the hands weren't doing all the preparing beforehand and the tidying up after. And then there was the day they picked. The shortest day. Another big joke. Like they wouldn't let us have an hour more than they could get away with. Ha ha. I bet the masters laughed at that, the bastards.

Not that I had ever been to a house like that, or a party like that, and I would have hated it. It wasn't so much like this in the city, but still everything seemed to stop on that one day, and the food was better, and Kal didn't find fault or not as much. I mean, there was still all the troupe to get fed and washed up after, but at least Batiaire wasn't around, and that always felt like a holiday. After we'd eaten there'd be dancing, and when people got tired there'd be songs, and stories, and I'd tuck myself into a quiet corner of the big warm kitchen, and watch everyone, and listen to everything that was sung and said, and store it away for when I needed it. As the night wore on, and people got sleepy, they'd curl up in their corners, and I would go out into the yard, in case there were fireworks somewhere in the city, and I could catch a peep of them. And you'd wish each other well, and the best for the year that was coming, although you knew, really, that things didn't change much for people like us – the work went on, and didn't stop, and eventually you got older and ran out of steam. Still, the wish was there. And this year it had come true.

Well, there was always going to be a big party at our town, wasn't there? Or more like a hundred fair-sized parties. I knew Kal was worried that things might get out of hand, and I'd seen her and Crith busy for a good few weeks beforehand, talking to the people they most trusted from the other bands, making sure that there'd be a few people sober and keeping an eye on things. But you could hardly stop people from celebrating, could you? This year there really was something to celebrate.

This year the world really had turned upside-down.

Por was excited; her first real party, I guess. Tella – well, you could see that she was missing her folks, and when Por asked what she would usually be doing, she didn't say much, and we didn't push. We had made our peace, more or less, the three of us, and my time these days was spent with Tella and Por. I say more or less because I still didn't like how blunt Tella was with Por sometimes, how impatient, and I didn't always like how Por did more than her fair share of the work, or so it seemed to me. But I bit my lip and kept it buttoned and tried not to say anything. Thinking about it now, I suppose they had to put up with a fair amount from me. The endless talking, for one thing. I can't help myself. I always liked to talk. I always liked to tell a tale. It's not good for a hand, and Kal tried to belt it out of me, but I have never been able to stop myself. Never.

So everyone had been busy, for weeks it seemed, not just with their ordinary jobs, but with all sorts of secret tasks. There'd been hammering and building here and there, and extra cooking from saved food, and people quickly hiding things away from other people. When the three of us met, mid-morning, as we usually did, we each of us handed out small presents we'd made for each other. Por turned out to have a gift for whittling, and gave Tella a figure of the little blue water goddess that she liked to pray to, and I got a dance-fighter in full flight. I had laid my hands on some proper sweets, and saved them, and put them into two little bags that I made from some pretty cloth I'd found. Tella had made these beautiful bracelets. Por's had blue and gold beads on it. Tella said those were the colours of friendship, and whether it was true or not, Por was so happy she could barely speak, and she just sat there, with the bracelet on her wrist, touching the little beads one by one with her finger tip, like they were the most precious things in this whole old world. I don't think Por had ever really owned anything of her very own before, not really. My bracelet had tiny pieces of metal polished so well that they looked like stars. I've worn it ever since. Here. Here it is. Yes, I know, it's beautiful.

I think we all felt shy then, so we set off wandering around the town, and what struck me, I think, now I try to remember that day, was how different we were in this old town of ours, from just how far afield we had all come. There were songs I'd never heard before – and the others had a hard time pulling me away from those sometimes – and kinds of dance and theatre that I'd never seen before, and stories told in dialects I could barely follow. And we spotted the places where there was too much drinking going on, and steered well clear.

Well, the sun set, and we made our way back to our part of town, and saw that a big space had been cleared not far from where Seff and Crith and Kal had their tents. A big white sheet had been hung up between two trees. There was a big fanfare, and people near that started hushing, and then Seffish appeared, with the other two behind her. I wouldn't say she was in her finery, because we didn't have anything like that, but somehow she seemed to have a special sort of sheen about her. Yes, yes, I know I was crazy about her, but it was for a reason. She opened her mouth to speak, and, all of a sudden, it was as if her voice was coming from everywhere around us.

I heard the next morning that this happened all around the camp, and stars it must have given some of those country bumpkins a bastard of a shock. Some of them were pretty rough, you know, hadn't seen much beyond their big fields or a few lanes around a homestead, and I bet they didn't know that the masters could do things like this. But they could, they could 'cast their voices from one place to another, so that you could hear someone talking from far away. I guess the masters must think that things like this are a secret, or that we can't understand, but what they never seem to realise is that we *make* everything. We make it all, and none of what they dream up could exist without us.

And Seffy spoke, spoke out loud to all of us, and told us how magnificent we were, and how hard we'd worked, and that we were the best people that had ever lived, and how much she loved us and admired us. Stars, how much I loved her back. "Hey," she said, "we are turning this world upside down. We are the rock of this old world, the bones, and we are rising, rising, and the whole land is following us. We have broken our fetters. We are taking back our children, as bright as stars and sweet as water."

Well, we were all joining in by then, and by the time we were done there wasn't a dry eye as far as I could see, and even Tella was having a big old weep into her hands. Por was bawling. But they weren't done yet. It was dark now, very dark, and then all of a sudden I saw pictures flickering on the big old sheet. It took me a moment, and then my mouth fell open. Stars, if those bastards hadn't somehow managed to find a way to bring the flicks to me here, miles from anywhere, sitting on the ground

by a shitty old tent. I clapped my hands together in glee, and Tella burst
out laughing.

"Hey," I said, "did you know anything about this?"

"No," she said. "Although I knew something was up."

Well, the show didn't last long, and it was just scraps of stuff stitched
together, but oh stars I love this sad old world when it looks that way,
sort of softened and filtered, and everything put into a good order and
making sense. I cried at one point, to think how clever people had been
to put all this together, and then I cried some more because to be honest
it wasn't that much, really, was it, and we all deserved so much more, and
so much better, and this was all we had. This was everything we had.

After that, well, the night was long, and the three of us, despite
everything, were young and strong and full of hope. What else do you do
in the face of the longest night but hold each other, love each other?
What else do you do but dance?

There was a reason she gave this talk when she did, of course, that Kal
made her give this talk. We all of us knew that there were too many of
us here, stuck alongside each other, and that there were deep hatreds.
Free against slave, yes, but others too. The town-hands despised the
country-hands. And then there was a mess of people from all over, with
different songs and dialects, like I said, and the ones from the north
didn't really like the ones from the south, and the ones from the south
didn't really trust the ones from the north, and everyone hated the
westerners because we all know they're slippery bastards. Sometimes it
seemed the only thing we agreed on was that we fucking hated the
masters. So that was what Seffy was meant to be. Something to agree on
that came not from hate but from love. It should have worked. It did
work, for a while.

But somehow, for all Kal's efforts, there always seemed to be trouble
brewing somewhere, some flash of anger, some old enmity stirred up
into a fight or worse. Crith said it was because people were bored, and
because there'd been a few more 'birds recently, and that made them
twitchy. She said they'd be better come the spring, when no doubt the
masters would be heading our way. That would concentrate the mind,
she said. But Kal was not consoled, and then one day I heard someone
saying to someone else that if she was Crith she wouldn't put up with
being in Seffy's shadow so much and who did Seffish think she was

anyway. Well, I took that one straight back to Kal. I did a lot of listening out for Kal, and carried a lot of tales her way. And she didn't like that one. She didn't like that one at all.

"Where are they getting these ideas from, Kal?" I asked.

"I dunno," she said, and she didn't like that, oh no.

"Is it true?" I said. "Is Crith fed up? Is she jealous of Seffy?"

She lifted her hand to shut me up, but she didn't answer, not straight away, and that gave me one bastard of a fright. Two halves of a whole. But what if that was just the story for the flicks, wasn't it? This, I thought, was what it felt like for the world to turn upside down.

"Don't be daft," said Kal. "Of course she isn't. This is Crith, Iss. One of us. One of our pals. Now fuck off," she said. "You must have something better to do."

I turned to go, grumbling, but then all of sudden she was next to me, her hand on my arm. "Hey," I said, shaking her off, "that's a bit much."

"Listen, Iss," she said, all soft and scary. "I know you like to tell a tale, but if I hear you passing this one around, you'll have more to worry about than you've ever dreamed of. You understand me?"

Well, I was a bit hurt by that, like she thought I didn't understand what a story can do, or, worse, that I didn't grasp what the stakes were. "Fuck off," I said.

"I mean it —"

"I mean it too. I'm not a child, you know, Kal. Not any more."

But the idea had been put into my head, and I'd bet into a lot of other heads too.

The Story of the Hand Who Liked to Sing

Once upon a time there was a hand who liked to sing, and who was very good at it. Now, sometimes the masters like this, because the masters like possessing beautiful things, after all, and spend a lot time getting us to make them, or else we are the beautiful thing that they own, which makes them feel like they are beautiful, because they think that owning something is the same as being it. And let's not forget that a hand with a talent can be worth a lot, after all, like a singer or an acrobat or a dancer or a fighter, and the masters like making money as much as they like having beautiful things, which is the source of most of our troubles if you think about it for a minute or two.

But sometimes the masters don't like it when we're beautiful, or can do beautiful things, because it doesn't seem right that we should do something better than they can, and they think that it spoils the order of things. They like order very much too. Well, that was the case with this hand and her master. This hand lived on a farm in the back of beyond, a real old hard mean place in the country, with a master who you would think was made of stone. They had a hard time eking a living out of that land, and that poor hand bore the brunt of it. That's nothing new, I know, but I think it's worth mentioning anyway, because it matters a lot when you're the one bearing it. Well, wherever you are, I think, you can try to find some joy in living, and I have seen the poorest of the poor smile and laugh and joke, and hold out their hand to give in fellow feeling. But that mean old master had never learned that trick, and, besides, I think she found that joy in being hard as the rock of the world, or harder. So that hand who loved to sing, and who was good at it, sang her songs in secret, whispered them to herself as she worked, songs she had learned when she was a little one, from someone who had loved her. But sometimes, just sometimes, the song was so strong within her that she thought she would burst, and then, in the dead of night, she would creep away from her bed by the door, and slip outside, and down to the old canal, where she would whisper her song to the water as it struggled past.

Well, one night, she was down there by the water, singing softly to herself a song that she had known from when she was small, a song about the love we can feel for everything around us, and the night was so lovely, the sky so dark and the stars so bright, that she could not help herself, and she let her voice loose, and she sang her heart out to the night.

When she was done, she heard someone clapping.

Well, that gave her one bastard of a fright. She peered into the darkness, but could not see anyone, so she called out, "Who's there?"

From the other side of the water, a voice called back, "Me!"

"Who's me?"

"No one you know," said the voice. "Someone who likes your singing. Can you sing me another?"

Well, at first the hand did not want to sing again, for fear that her master might hear her and beat her, but the voice said, "There's nobody here but you and me, and the wind will carry your words away from the house, so why not take this chance?"

"Take my chance?" said the hand.

"To sing as you would like to."

Well, that was something that the hand had often dreamed of, and after a moment or two she began to sing. She sang all the songs that she had learned and heard throughout her life, from when she was small and someone loved her, to odd songs she heard on market day, when she and her master made their rare old trips to the outside world. She sang into the darkness, across the water, and when she came to the end of all she had learned, she stopped.

There was silence.

"Are you there?" she called out.

"I'm here," said the voice. "Sing me another."

"I don't know any more," said the hand.

"Still," said the voice, "sing me another."

So the hand started to sing one of her songs again.

"No," said the voice. "Sing me something new."

Well, the hand did not know what to do. She didn't know any more songs.

"What should I sing about?" she said.

"Sing to me of the start of things," said the voice.

So the hand closed her eyes, and reached out so that she could feel the wind upon her arms, and she listened to the night sounds, and then she began to sing. And the song she sang was new to her, words and tune she had never heard before, and oh my if she was amazed at this, because she did not know that she had new songs inside her.

Here is what she sang:

71

> This is the rock, the rock of the world
> The bones upon which everything rests
> The channel for the water
> The container for the soil
> The surface for the air
> The stuff that stars are made of
> The first and the last
> That lies behind the smoke upon the mountain
> That lies beneath the streams and fields
> The rock of the world is all is everything

When she was done, she heard at first nothing but silence, and she wondered if this song, her song, the first she had made and not learned, was any good. Then the voice said, "You must come here, whenever you can, and sing new songs. The wind is listening, and the water, and all that is good in this hard old world. Come and sing to me, whenever you can. Sing me a new song."

So the hand did that, not every night, but whenever she could. She came down to the canal, and sang her songs to the water and the wind, although she never heard the voice again. But the water and the wind have carried her songs to every corner of this old world, and that is how we know them, and her songs were beautiful and tell the truth, and that is why we sing them.

Nine

Barely ten days passed before we realised that Oenith and her hand had gone. Slipped away in the dead of night; headed off – east, we thought, though we didn't send people after them. I think Kal wanted to – she said that they could cause us a lot of trouble if the masters laid hands on them, tell them all sorts of things we'd rather the masters didn't know – but nobody had the stomach to hunt down some of our own. *No great loss*, was the general feeling; after all, they were always causing trouble, fighting and hurting people. Yes, they might have come in handy should the masters turn up, but think about the harm they could do in the meantime. On the whole people were happier that they'd buggered off. I'd no idea what they were hoping to do; prey on unlucky travellers, I suppose, or else find a big country house and settle there until they killed each other. Nobody really missed them. The problem was they weren't the last, and better people went next.

As spring drew closer, more and more started to slip away. Bastard cowards. We all knew there was a big fight coming, that the masters would be heading our way soon enough, and they were legging it before that happened. Stars, some people are stupid. Our strength was in our numbers. Heading off in bands of two dozen – well, you were easier to pick off, weren't you? Did they think they were just going to be left alone? The masters couldn't have that. Couldn't leave some of us wandering about, free.

Some people, though, didn't fade away in the middle of the night. They came and spoke to Seffy and said *Sorry, but...* I felt for some of these. They weren't from this part of the world. They had been pulled away from all over, dragged off to work the big farms, thinking once they were there that they didn't have long left. And then this second chance had come along, this new lease of life... They were thinking of the places they had left behind, people too, of course: loves and little ones and others. Now they knew they were going to live longer, they wanted to see them again. So they'd come and say sorry to Seffy, and then they'd go. And then there were the free-folk, who'd never fitted in, but had ended up here, with us. And they'd lived off us all this time, but now that the trouble was coming, they were packing up and going. Off to the big cities, some of them said. Perhaps they had family there they could beg off. Poor relations, kept at the back of the house, charity cases. Imagine picking that instead of being here, with us, free. People make some fucking strange choices.

Well, Kal was furious about all this, but what could she do? We could hardly force any of these people to stay, could we? She became obsessed with the idea that there were spies amongst us, sent by the masters, to stir up trouble amongst us, and she fretted about it all the time, how she could spot them, how we could find them out. Well, on the whole, I think we were well able to do all that under our own steam – people are like that, aren't they? But Kal was the brains, wasn't she? She said that's what she would do, and so she had no doubt about it. It was a hard time, tense, unhappy, and I think we were all just hanging on, hoping it would end soon, that whoever wanted to go would get on with it, and then the rest of us would know where we stood, and could get on with facing the spring and whatever that was going to bring. When a big band of free-folk, a couple of hundred, went off, we thought, *Oh surely this is the end of it.*

Then Crith left.

That day, the day Crith broke the news, was a shocker. Awful. I cried so much my face was raw. I hid away until I knew I could face people again, and the first person I ran into was Por.

"Where the fuck have you been?" she yelled at me. Well, I'd never heard that from Por before.

"Lay off," I said.

"Lay off? Don't you know what's going on?"

"Of course I know. Crith –"

"Not Crith, you fucking idiot!" she said. "Tella! Tella's going with them!"

She didn't even try to deny it.

"Don't argue with me, Iss. I've made the decision and that's that."

"It's not her," said Por, from behind my shoulder. "It's that bastard witch she brought here with her –"

"Don't call her things like that, Por," Tella said firmly. "You know I hate it."

"I don't understand," I said. "I thought you were finding your feet here. I thought you were getting used to us."

"I was..." she said. "I was. But this is a chance, don't you see? A chance to get back to normal. Back to, well..."

"Civilisation, she said," said Por.

"Did she," I said, and looked at Tella, who to give her credit was ashamed.

"I'm not cut out of this," she said, defensively. "You two – you can make something here. But not me. I'm not cut out for this." As if saying it twice would make it true.

I had one last go. "If it's *her* making you do this," I nodded towards the tent, where the old woman was snoring, "you don't owe her anything. You brought her here, saved her life, and that's all you have to do."

"It's not her," Tella said. "Not just her. I'm scared here, Iss. People don't trust me, not really. They know I'm not one of them... Not one of you. I have to get back to a place where I belong. Where I feel safe."

"Safe," I said, thinking: *They burned your fucking farm down.* "All right."

"Here," said Por. "Take this. Keep it. You never meant it anyway." And she pulled the bracelet Tella had made off her wrist, and threw it on the ground, and ran away.

Tella stooped slowly to pick it up, but I was in there first.

"She'll be sorry she did that," I said.

"I don't know about that," said Tella, and, gently, firmly, took it from my hands.

And that was that. Crith was leaving, with a good part of our people, and when she set off, Tella walked off with her.

You know, I only got half the story from Kal, who stayed pretty tight-lipped about the whole thing, but I did get that, and I filled in the rest for myself as best as I could, which is, after all, what I'm good at. Maybe the story going round that she was fed-up of being second to Seffy was true, maybe telling it made it come true, but the simple fact was that Crith had had enough. I didn't know until then that Crith was from the north. She'd been down amongst us for a long time, and she never mentioned it. Well, if you think you've no chance of ever going home you try to put it out of your mind, don't you? That's one reason I've never talked much about what happened at this time. Because this ramshackle army, and the town by the Big Lock – that's the only place I'd ever think of calling home, and that's never coming back, is it? It's gone for good.

So Crith had had a home once, it turned out, and now she wanted to

75

go and see it again. She was tired, she said; tired of fighting, tired of living this way. She was getting on. She wanted some peace. Well, I'm sure you can guess what Kal thought of that, and I'm not saying it loud because this here is quite a nice place and you don't want to hear how creative Kal could be when she was angry. And I would guess too that while she didn't much mind always coming second after Seffy in the hearts of the rest of us, she did mind coming second after Kal where Seffy was concerned. What I mean by that is, Seffy always took Kal's advice. You just did that, you see – you did what Kal said, because you knew how smart she was. And Crith – well, what lover would like that? What lover would like always to be placed second? That's what I think happened, in the end. Seff loved Crith, but she trusted Kal's judgement more. And that was never going to work. Stars, though – why are we so broken? Why are we so faulty? Why couldn't they have made it work, somehow? Even now, a part of me resents it. They were our heroes, or supposed to be our heroes. We were little people. We just wanted them to be that bit better than us. So that they could save us.

But they weren't, which was our mistake, if I'm being honest with myself, and that was that. Crith left as soon as she could, and she took nearly half of us with her, and Tella not least.

Winter was dreary after that. Sort of hopeless, the way it always is after the big festival, with nothing to look forward to but the next day's work. And we had plenty of that, keeping ourselves fed, and trying to prepare ourselves for the spring, when the masters would come. Everyone was learning to fight, even ones much littler than me, and of course Por and I were easily big enough.

Well, I suppose I had always dreamed that somehow I could dance like my heroes, but the truth is that some people have the knack and some people have two flat feet, and the best I can say is that I would like to think that watching my efforts at least lightened a few hearts in the middle of that miserable winter. Seffy would come to see, she even worked with me a few times, but everyone including me knew that when the fight came, I would not be right at the front. If the masters' soldiers reached wherever I was, it was over.

Por, meanwhile, was a natural. Whoever would have thought? She chucked herself into the training. Seffy took a special interest, began to train her personally. And the dancing unlocked something in Por. She stood taller, straighter. I think, even despite our short rations, she was eating more than she ever had in her life. She had found her place. She had found the reason to live. And perhaps there was some anger in this too – at what her life had been before she got here, all the years of fear and work and living off scraps, all the years she'd been afraid. I was glad she was angry about it all at last, and I was glad, most of all, how it didn't pull her all out of shape. This life was the making of Por.

Kal, meanwhile, chucked herself into smoking out the spies amongst us. I said she was obsessed, and it got very bad around this time. Every week or so she pulled out a couple of people, and they got questioned, and some of them got sent away, and some of them went off in anger. I think she made a big mistake here, causing a lot of the ill feeling she was trying to root out. But she was sure, so sure, that the masters had people in our midst, spreading rumours, telling lies, trying to make us quarrel amongst ourselves. Maybe she was right. But sometimes, watching her go about her business, and listening to what people said about her behind her back, I wasn't sure whether or not she was doing the masters' work for them.

We knew that this time at our camp, where we had been happy, on the whole, was coming to an end. But winter had one last cruel surprise up her sleeve. One bright morning, one of those startling days that have all the light of summer but none of the warmth, a ragged little band of travellers was spotted coming south towards us. We sent out scouts to watch them, make sure they weren't going to be trouble, and while they weren't, the news they brought was.

There were about two dozen of them, and they were all known to us. Every single one of them had marched out with Crith. And these were, as far as they knew, the only ones left.

Well, when news of their arrival reached us, me and Por dashed down to get news. And, hope against hope, there she was – our Tella. Thin, and dirty, and with a wild look in her eyes. We pulled her away from the rest, into the safety of our arms.

"We were ambushed," she said. "It was like they knew we were coming."

I thought, *Kal will want to hear about that.*

"They killed and killed and killed. Crith fought so hard. I have never seen anyone fight so hard... When it was all over, some of us, they went to the soldiers and said that they were free-folk. But they killed them too. They killed everyone they could lay their hands on. Little ones, old ones..." She sobbed, suddenly, a desperate gasp. "I didn't like her, you know, the old woman. But she didn't deserve that."

Por held her while she cried, and I clasped one of her hands. When she was done, she sat up. She reached into her pocket, and pulled out the little bead bracelet. Por let her put it back in place on her arm.

"I'm sorry," Tella said, as she put it there. "I should never have left. We were better together. None of us should ever have left."

Later, I left Tella and Por asleep in each other's arms, and crept back to my own tent, near to Kal and Seffy. I heard Seffy weeping too, crying out Crith's name, but softly, Kal holding her, and hushing her, because they couldn't let the rest of us hear them. They couldn't let the rest of us know that they were just the same as us.

The Story of the Hand Who Got Very Lost

Once, in the kindly north-country where the grass is green and the spring flowers bright, there was a hand who liked to walk about, a lot more than perhaps she should, and a lot more than her master liked, if the truth be told. But since she worked so well in the day, her master, who was not the worst sort, let her walk, as long as she swore that she would always return by nightfall, and would not sleep beneath the stars but be back in her own bed near the house. And the hand saw this was a fair enough offer, and kindly and wisely made, and made that promise, since her heart would have broken without these walks, out amongst the spring flowers and the green leaves of the trees and the swift cold streams that ran down from the snowy mountains. And, when the day's work was done, and the supper cleared, she would take her walk, and always, always, return to her bed that night.

Over the years, this hand had three children. One of them was lost early, and the second of them the master sold on, and the third – the sweetest and brightest of them all – she was allowed to keep. And she loved now to be at her humble home, near this child, watching her blossom and flower and grow, but still, at the end of the day, the outside called to her, and she would walk out beneath the trees beside the swift cold streams and taste, for a little time, how it might feel to be free. But now when she returned her arms would be full of flowers, for her sweet bright child.

One evening, at the very height of summer, the hand kissed her child goodnight and rocked her to sleep. She was tired, because the day had been long, and the summer festival had been days in the making, and hours in the clearing. Looking down at the sleeping child, she thought for a moment that she might simply lie down next to her and go to sleep, but the room was hot, and her head was busy, and she knew the walk would do her good, so instead she went out to wander beneath the old green trees.

Who knows what happened next? We are not superstitious people, after all, and the tales of gods and spirits and genii that the masters tell each other are a source of great amusement amongst us, if the truth be told, since we know that the rock of the world binds us all to it, and nothing lies beyond. Perhaps one day there will be an explanation for all this, but that, as things stand, is beyond my power. But you should know that as the hand walked beneath the trees, she heard a strange humming and singing, and she stopped to listen, and she wondered what could make such a lovely sound. She saw the path leading home, and she even took a step or two along it, but something about that song drew her to it, and she came off the path to find out who these singers were, and how they made such a beautiful song.

At last the trees seemed to draw back, and the hand reached a clearing. And there, under the canopy of trees, was a small hut. Its door stood open, and a bright light shone out upon the ground, and the singing, it seemed, came from inside. Slowly, the hand crept forwards and into the hut. When she passed the threshold, the door closed behind her, and the singing stopped, and the lights went dim. She rattled at the handle, but the door was now locked, and there isn't much you can do to locks and bars and chains, as we all know, so she sat down upon the floor, and waited.

That night was, as I say, the shortest. There was a window in one wall, and the hand saw the sky outside go dark, and looked out at the stars, and worried at how late she was. But since the door did not open there was nothing to be done, so she lay down and went to sleep. And when she woke, the sky outside was bright again, and she tried the door, which opened, and she went out into a bright summer morning.

Well, of course, she ran all the way home. She was badly afraid. She knew that she had broken a promise to her master, a promise that she would always sleep in her own bed close to the house, and she knew that she would be punished, and that the way to punish her was through the bright sweet child that she had been allowed to keep.

When she came at last to the wall around the house, she knew that something strange was happening. The house, the master's house, had grown overnight, with a whole new wing at one side. At first she thought that she had come the wrong way, and this was a different house, but no – she knew the door, and she knew the old buildings, and she knew that this was her home. Well, she wasted no time running round to the place where the hands lived, and there too she saw changes: more low cabins, and more people. And there, sitting on the step of the house where she had promised always to sleep, was an old woman.

She knew at once who this old woman was – she was her child, the sweetest and the brightest of them all, that she had been allowed to keep, and seeing that all the years of her life had passed, and were lost, never to return, the hand's heart became hard as the rock of the world, but the grief it held was still too great, and her heart shattered into tiny pieces, scattering on the ground. And the old woman, that sweet bright child, walking that way, saw the fragments glistening there, and said how many flowers there were that spring, more than she had ever seen before in her long years. And that was the end of that.

Ten

So. Tella. She was changed, of course. I think that even when the farm was taken and everyone she loved was killed, Tella had to keep on telling herself that there'd been a mistake, that somehow if the masters had known they were free-folk they would not have done what they did. But this – this massacre – she couldn't deny that. She had been shown, up close and as clear as possible, that she didn't count. That she was worthless. And that was the end of that. She joined Por in training; training to fight. She didn't have Por's grace and ease, but she was tougher, better fed when she was small, and there was a hard edge in her eyes when she fought. You could see she would never surrender, not again. She'd fight till she dropped, or till they held her arms behind her back, and if that happened she would start kicking and biting.

It wasn't long before I realised the plan had changed, some decision had been made. Something had stirred in us at the news of Crith's death, and the killing of so many. We weren't content to sit here any longer, waiting for the masters to come. Once grief and shock were past, we reached anger. We wanted revenge. Kal sensed the mood change. Scouts went out more often now; came back in the dead of night with whispered messages. The 'casters were busy too, and I couldn't crack the code, no matter how hard I tried. And I did try, finding reasons to go their way whenever I could, listening as I went past.

Kal came to me one night. "Heard you've been hanging around the 'casters again," she said. "If I didn't know you better, I'd think you were trying to sniff out my secrets."

"Wouldn't dare, Kal."

"No?"

"No," I said, because when she made a decision about whether one of us had turned to the masters, she didn't listen to reason. "All I want is to know what's going on."

She sat down beside me with a bump. She'd never had what you'd call a young face, because work and worry make you go old quick, don't they, but these days she looked like she was carrying the rock of the world on her back. Nobody should do that, or think they have to. I sat looking at that old stone face of hers, and I thought how much I loved her, the hard old miserable old witch.

"Kal," I said. "You're not on your own. You'll never be. You'll always have me."

She gave me a sharp look, and I could see her trying to decide whether or not to tell me to button it, or to shut my yap, but the moment passed.

"Yep," she said, after a while. "I know."

We sat and watched the campfires.

"We're leaving in a day or two," she said. "Had you worked that out, my sharp-eyed Iss?"

Well, I'd had a hunch, but nothing that you might call definite information.

"I sort of guessed."

"Yes, you would," she said.

"Is it going to be a big fight?"

"Pretty big," she said. "Don't worry, you won't be in the middle of it."

"I'm not useless," I said.

"At that," she said, "you are."

Which was fair enough and, to be fair to her, she wasn't dismissing me completely.

"Besides, if this gamble pays off," she said, "I have other plans for you. But you'll need to learn to keep your yap shut."

Her usual telling-off, but her heart wasn't in it. As she stood up, I said, "What about Por and Tella?"

She gave a funny old smile. "Our twin dancers," she said. "The new Crith and Seffy. Well, they're going to get their first taste of real fighting."

"Second," I said.

"What?"

"Tella's been there already. And Por too, if you count what happened at the house where she lived."

Slowly, Kal nodded. "Second," she agreed. "It won't be the last."

So we packed up, and said goodbye to the camp by the lock. I was sad to go, because this was the place where, if only in moments here and there, I had known what it was to be happy, to have a home, to have company and fellowship and friendship. But nothing lasts forever, not even peace and freedom. Especially not peace and freedom.

We headed north, towards the masters.

The land we passed through was hushed, and stripped bare. Whatever homes had been here stood empty, their owners afraid that they would find no mercy at our hands. They had good reason, I suppose. There wasn't much pity in us now, except for each other, who were, as far as I was concerned, more cherished than ever before. And it seemed the masters felt the same way. The lands around were ruined, scorched, left so we couldn't use anything. Kal sent round orders not to drink from the wells before checking the water was safe. Good job too.

Well, the fight came at last, near a crossroads where two big roads met, and it was as bloody and as vicious as you might expect. Bitter, bitter, hardened by life and the promise of freedom snatched away, our fighters were ready and willing. So we won, we beat the masters on their ground, again, and the way north lay open to us. But I don't know, it didn't seem much of a victory to me. When Por and Tella came back from that day they were different again. They had gone past me somehow, started on a road I would never follow them along. I knew they'd killed, and I knew they'd killed more than once, and were ready to go again. And I was at the back, someone to protect, not fight alongside.

They got the chance to kill again within a few short weeks. Seffish pushed us onwards, further north, deep into the masters' country, and we fought the bloodiest battle (well, the bloodiest battle yet) and we won that too. The way was clear, now, to strike the capital. Anger drove us, and the need for revenge. I thought, and I heard many say, *Crith should be here.* Winning would never again feel like winning; or, at least, not for a very long time. And my friends? My friends were turning into strangers.

I think that if we had forged on, we might well have taken the capital, the mood we were all in. Or perhaps that hot fury would have driven us to terrible mistakes. Who knows? Guessing what might have been is a storyteller's job, yes, perhaps, but all I want to do right now is set this story down as it happened, or how it seemed to me at the time. I'll leave the happy endings for someone else, for another time, another place, another world. Still, sometimes I think about how it would have been, to take that grand old city of greying stone and drive the masters from their big houses, and tear down the walls and set all the hands there free. To sit in those halls and make our own world, here, on the rocks and bones of the old one. Would we have made a better job of it? So far, we had done all right. Hadn't we?

But we didn't go on. We stopped. We took up a position outside the city, on the hills all around. There weren't enough of us, not really, to lay a siege, and the masters had learned from their mistakes, and sent small parties out to fret at us, chipping away at what we had. I think, perhaps, that Kal was waiting to hear whether there were any more of us coming down from the north, now the winter was ending; parties who had not made it south yet, or perhaps (hope against hope) survivors from Crith's troupe... But we were deep in enemy country now, and the 'casts stayed dead. We were all there was. Yes, there were many of us, enough, I'd bet, to make the masters lying in their beds at night sweat in fear. But this was the end of us. There would be no more.

And Seffy, I knew, wanted to go no further.

"We've won," she said to Kal. "Or as good as."

Kal, I knew, didn't think so. Kal wanted to gamble one more time.

"Won? There city is still there – look! They're in there, biding their time, waiting for us to fall at the last barrier."

Seffy did look, down at that grey city that lay in the palm of her hand, but she wasn't tempted. Seff wasn't tempted by power. She liked to feel strong, and she liked to feel free, and the dance gave her that. She killed when the need arose, but she never got that taste for it so many do. Perhaps if Crith had been there... But Crith was gone, and dead.

"I'm looking. They're stuck. We have them where we want them. Besides – they'll defend that place like nowhere else they've defended. It's their heart, isn't it? You know how they talk about it. Their eternal city."

"So we finish it," Kal said. "We make them see that they're not immortal."

"Even if we did it, the comeback would be terrible."

"Where from? The heart, you said. We'd have ripped the heart from them."

"Kal," said Seffy. "Surely we can find a way to live in peace?"

"In *peace*? They won't leave us in peace, Seff! They can't."

"I don't see why not –"

"Because we're the living proof of the limits of their power. Their peace, their settlement, their wealth and comfort – it all rests on us. Lies on our shoulders. We carry them, like the rock of the world resting on us."

"I still don't see, Kal, why they can't just ignore us. Let us be. We could send messengers, what do they call them, ambassadors. Say to them – we won't come no further. We won't pass this point."

"Because as long as some of us are free, we contradict their peace. We say that their way of life isn't the best way, the only way, like they say it is. And their hands, they'll look beyond the border at us, and they'll know we're there, and some of them will want to be with us, and run away, or want to stay where they are but be free."

"So you think they want to finish us for good."

"Of course they do. They can't let us live and let live. So I say we finish what we started. We go on. We take the city, and we make ourselves its masters. Better still, we get rid of masters for good."

"They won't give up without a fight."

"Worth it," said Kal.

Seffy said, "You sound like Oenith."

"I'm starting to think Oenith had a point."

"So you want to kill them all?"

Kal said, "I don't want to kill anyone."

I'll never forget what Seffy said next. "It isn't you, Kal," she said, "who does the killing."

Well, the look Kal gave her then was exactly how she looked at me before she belted me, and I thought: *She wouldn't dare, not Seffy*. She didn't, of course. She reached out to cup her hand around Seff's cheek. She had this tender streak, Kal, didn't she, when she thought no one was looking. She held Seff's cheek in her hand, and then she pulled it back. Stood up. Looked at the sky. The sun was up. The first big heat of the year would be coming soon, and then summer would be upon us and we'd all be sweltering. No escape from that.

"Spring is coming," she said. "What a joke."

Oh Kal, how I loved you, but there was something broken about you that you couldn't mend, and you shared that around as much as anything else. For all your hard work and your sharp fierce love, you could blight the strongest growth. And some of us weren't particularly strong. We were very ordinary. I understand, Kal, I do, but it was very hard sometimes, to try to grow even a little under your watch.

Yes, I understand why Kal was the way she was. The masters spoil everything they touch; they turn the world upside down. It's not right to fear the spring, the source of life and growth. It's not right.

Part 3

SPRING

Eleven

With the spring, the 'birds came.

New ones, said the experts amongst us; types and styles they had never seen before. Looked like the masters had been busy over the winter too, and they hadn't forgotten us. No, they were not going to forget about us, not ever, not as long as we were still out there, being free.

We did send ambassadors down to the city, like Seffy said we should, to make our offer of peace and separation. We sent two of them down there, one white morning when the first flowers were coming through. Didn't hear back, and we began to think we never would. But they did come back, in the end: one of 'em blinded, the other with no tongue. That was enough to be able to give the masters' message, though. *Surrender. Completely. Or not one of you will live to the end of the summer.*

"I said," Kal said, grimly, "that we should have finished them off."

But that moment had gone, and whatever future that might have brought, down there in the masters' city, was gone too, and now there was the present to live with.

From where we right now, it's easy to think we were done for at this point, and I imagine you're wondering why we didn't know it. So it's important to remember that there were still very many of us. Still enough to hold our own against whatever the masters could throw at us. But right now we lacked a purpose, other than to remain free. That was enough for some of us. Not all.

"People will leave," Kal told Seffy. "Drift away. Take their chances. They saw our messengers, and if they didn't, they've heard. They know the masters are coming, and they'll want to get away before that happens. What do you want, Seffy? I told you what we should do, and you said no. So what do you want?"

Not to be the one everybody looked to, I thought. But that was how it was. That was Seffy's job in all of this.

"We'll go back south," said Seffy, at last. "Back to our own lands. We can be peaceful there. Start the farms up again. Live alongside each other, in peace."

"And you think the masters will let us?"

"We'll draw a line. A border. Us on this side, you on that side. Leave us alone and we'll leave you alone. That's what we should have done to start with. Taken our country. Left them to their country. So we'll do that now."

Kal didn't answer at first, but eventually she nodded. "If that's what you want," she said. But she must have been thinking what I was thinking. *The 'birds can fly over borders.*

Still, we headed south again, back the way we'd come in the first place.

What happened next was a mess, a downright mess, and it's only because the masters are the way they are that we weren't all dead within the week. We knew, through our 'casters and from our scouts, that a new general had been placed over the masters' forces. Crassiaire. Yes, did you know this was how she made her name? How she made her fortune too before she went back to the capital and started there. People forget about this part of her career, the way it all ended for her. They just remember her hanging. Well, I try not to forget how she started, with everything that happened after the next few months. I try not to forget that Crassiaire's ambition all ended up with her being executed as a traitor. Yes, yes, a long time ago, you're saying, but what matters to me is that I outlived her. For all her power, and her wealth, and her triumphs, a greasy kitchen hand outlived her. I'll take that victory, you know. I'll take it. Because there isn't much else.

All that was in the future. All we knew about Crassiaire at this point was that she was young, and hungry, and she wanted us dead. The first thing she did was come at us from above.

Well, I know we're all used to seeing this kind of thing these days, but not back then. Back then 'birds were something that flew overhead to check the lie of the land, find out what was going on so that the soldiers could get in there. They weren't part of the actual battle. It took one flyover to send us into panic. Shooting down at us. We went this way and that, everywhere. All of us sent into a spin: fighters and hard old farm-hands and little uns and oldies alike. And it's only because one of Crassiaire's captains jumped the gun and wasn't in the right place at the right time that we got away. That's what we worked out later, at any rate. The idea had been to panic us, drive us off in one direction to hit the nearest canal, and have the rest of the army lying in wait for us there. But they weren't there. They'd gone off. The captain had the bright idea of ambushing us on the way, but we came down to the canal a different way. By the time she'd realised what was happening and turned her people round, we'd taken the boats and were on our way west.

You know what happens next, I think. It was part of the legend of Crassiaire. The story of ruthlessness that she built up around her as she took the eternal city by storm. No? You've never heard? Well, perhaps that legend hasn't lasted as long as Crassiaire would have liked, and I can't say I'm going to shed any tears over that. She had the captain executed and she gathered together that captain's army, and had one in ten of them shot. Poor bastards, they'd only been following orders, after all. But that's what the masters are like. Discipline, they called it. At least a firing squad is quick. That's your reward, when you're free. Ending it all quick. The rest of Crassiaire's army drew back, and she had some explaining to do to her own masters, I should imagine.

Well, we didn't know any of this at the time, of course, only that we'd had a bastard lucky escape, and that we needed to get away as quickly as we could. The barges helped, shifting some of us westwards, the rest following in the trucks or at a quick march. We left a few hundred behind to cover our escape.

We lived in terror of the skies after that – always looking up and cursing the daytime. We didn't know, of course, what I know now, that it wasn't a trick the masters could use all the time back then. Crassiaire had bet everything on that one attack from above, and one of her underlings had buggered it up. Good news for us, if we'd known this, but as it was we were scared at what each new day would bring. Seffy and Kal pushed us on, hard; Seffy cursing the day we'd ever come so far north; Kal, I know, regretting the day we'd turned away from that hard city to take a different course. They never resolved that between them and although they never quarrelled about it again, or not so I heard, and you can bet that I was listening, it must have rankled. Chip, chip, chip, the stones are falling down. Things crumble and fall apart.

Our cover didn't make it. A dozen, maybe, caught up with us, giving news of the mop-up. Crassiaire hadn't shown much mercy. Piled up the dead bodies in great heap, and strung up the living prisoners on forked logs in a great circle around them. Set fire to the bodies. We'd seen the smoke from the north, wondered what it was. Now we knew. Now we knew too that they really had meant what they'd said when they'd sent our ambassadors back. They wanted us all dead. And they wanted a spectacle too. They wanted an example.

The day after this happened, Tella went to Kal. Demanded that she got to fight the next time around. I wish I'd been there to hear that. All I saw afterwards was Tella, furious.

"She said I was a kid! A kid! Like I've not proven myself. But it's not that, is it? It's because I'm not one of you."

"Eh?" I said.

"Not a hand."

Por and I looked at each other. I'll be honest, I'd more or less forgotten that about Tella. She was one of us now.

"She's crackers, you know that?" Tella went on. "Sees threat everywhere."

"To be fair," I said, "she's got good reason, hasn't she?"

"But me? What do I have to do, eh? I can't change how I was born. I can't change where I came from!"

Nor could none of us, I thought, though I didn't say it. What was the use of quarrelling at this point? Now, more than ever, we had to pull together. We had been pushed off course, much further west than we wanted, slowing us down as we headed back to the lands we'd come from. And we didn't know when the 'birds would come past again.

I did what I always did when one of us was in a state like this. I came up with a story. An old one, a really old one, but not one that Tella would ever have heard, because truth be told, she wasn't one of us. She'd not been born one of us. She wouldn't have heard these old stories, would she? Someone had to tell them to her, and there was only us. Me and Por, who loved her.

The Story of the Dance

Well, as you know the masters do not think that we can create anything, but say instead that they are the source of all things that are ingenious, and that we are there to build and make and through our work turn their ideas into reality. I hope that by now I have shown how that is not true. And if you are not yet convinced by this, let me tell you about the dance. The one thing that proves beyond all measure how untrue this is, is the dance. It is ours, and ours alone, and we made it, and we refined it, and we taught it to each other.

It started as a dance, nothing more. Even the smallest child, hearing music, will bend and sway and tilt to the sound. Some of us get no better, that's for sure, our feet are flat and while we might like to dance like the best of us, we can only admire. But we understand. Dancing is the body set free. That is why the masters hate the dance, in their hearts, and when the found they could not stop it, they stole it, and made us dance for them, to make them rich or should I say richer.

Because the dance is a weapon, our oldest weapon. Because where there are masters there will be a hand trying to get away, and throughout the long hard years on this old hard world we have taught ourselves, again and again, ways to get away. Whether singing our songs to the wind, or picking the masters' pockets, or taking our time at our tasks, or doing them badly, we have found these little cracks of freedom wherever we can, and we have tried to pass them on as best we can. And this is what the dance is: a piece of freedom, passed on between us.

Watch the dancer. Watch her move. Watch her kick and spin and jump and fly. In the moment, in the movement, she is free. She is not bound to the rock of the world, she is not fettered or shackled or yoked. She is in flight. Her body is hers and hers alone. She belongs to nobody but herself. She is her own master, and she has the means to defend herself. You cannot get past her. She anticipates your moves. She is there before you. She puts herself between you and what she loves. (Oh yes, yes, no wonder the masters hate the dance. No wonder they stole it. No wonder they stuck the best of our dancers into compounds, and put them to work for them, and bought them and sold them, and placed bets on them. Because they know they cannot stop the dance. The best they can ever do is subvert it, steal it, thieve it, because that it what the masters are. They are thieves.)

You might say, this is not much, but this is all we have. When you come at us with whips and with pistols, we have to defend ourselves somehow. We have to put ourselves between you and the ones that we love. And we only have our bodies. We only have the dance. Sometimes it's fast enough. Sometimes it's nothing in the face of everything against us. But it is ours, ours alone, and it is something that we made.

Yes, something that we made. But the problem with our creations is that they do not last. They are written in space, not time, fleeting, passing, whispered to each other on the winds and on the waters. The songs, the stories, the dance – they are not fixed in stone, except upon us, upon our bodies. Because we are the rock, the rock of the world, and our memories endure. Somehow, they endure.

Twelve

The 'birds didn't attack us from the sky again, but they did send us messages. Sent us news, you might say, of those of us they had captured – scouts, or people who had gone off, or who had been too slow behind us. When I say messages, I mean. Well. Let's say these messages were written on the body. Imagine that, falling from above. You've got to wonder about the masters sometimes. And people wonder why we didn't give up.

We got other messages too, more directly, via the 'casters, instructions for surrender. I was hanging around, wasn't I ever, when one of these came through. Crassiaire herself speaking, giving orders in that voice the masters use: sharp, brisk, and assuming obedience. *Give up now. There is and can be no escape.* Well, I don't know much about negotiating, but I can't say she made it seem a particularly attractive offer. I took to saying that after every 'cast: "That's great, but what's in it for me?" Kal was ready to snap at me, but it made Seffy laugh, so I got away with it. Heard Seff saying it herself a few times. That was a high point. You like to think you've said something memorable.

Since we weren't being offered terms, there wasn't much point in listening really, so we changed the channels that we used. They found us and 'casted on those. We changed them again. They found us. Kal got angry at one point, kicked a 'caster into the dust. Well, it wasn't like we were using them much any more, not since the early days when we'd been gathering together. There was nobody else coming to join us, not now. We were all that was left. Still, we gathered up the pieces because everything comes in useful by and by.

The last assault had pushed us further west than we would have liked into that big peninsula, and I knew that Kal was eager to get us back out and on track for the south country. Problem was, we didn't know what lay ahead, and Seffy was getting twitchy about sending out scouts that didn't come back. We needed all the fighters we had. So round and round they went, her and Kal, never quite making the decision that was needed. This was why we missed Crith. Somehow between them those three always broke the deadlock. With two it was just head-to-head.

One night I went to Kal and made my offer. She looked at me as if

I'd sprouted wings. Wish I had. They'd've come in handy.

"No chance," she said.

"No, Kal, listen," I said. "Hear me out –"

"I've heard you. You're not going."

"Why not?"

"Cause you'll trip over your own feet and get yourself caught, that's why."

"No I won't," I said. "You know I won't. I'm good at sneaking about, me. The times I got past you and you never knew –"

"You're not too big for me to belt you."

"Yes I am. And I don't care what you say, Kal. I'm off. Tella's coming with me."

I did think then that she was going to hit me, but she just sort of fell back against the ground. "Doubt I can stop you," she said. "And at least you'll be out of my way for a bit."

Well, I wasn't going to get anything else out of her, so I took that as permission, and even as what the masters would call a blessing.

So Tella and I slipped off early one morning, not telling anyone else what we were doing. No, not even Por, because she would have wanted to come too, and three was too many, and, besides, she was a fighter now, getting to be one of the best, and she was needed for that.

So, like I say, we had been pushed west a way, into that big peninsula, and I knew Kal was worried about us getting trapped in there, and was keen to get back on track as quickly as possible. What we needed was some news about where the masters were and what they were up to. So that was where me and Tella were heading. A long walk, and slow, keeping to cover as much as we could. Funny, though, it was nice, in a way: spring was taking hold and there were all the small flowers in the cracks of the rocks. Tella knew their names, or most of them. Country knowledge. I could only tell them apart by colour, until she taught me what they were called. Still remember some of them, even now, after so long, little white starflowers and pale blue crowns. How do things stay so pretty in the face of everything else?

At last we came over the top of the last hill, and could look down into the valley that led back into the mainland. There we saw a vast hive of activity: ditch-digging, fence-raising,

I said, "It's a wall. They're putting up a wall."

Tella said, "Nothing gets past you, does it?"

I said, "Let me go down there and set fire to it."

Tella said, "We have to let Kal and Seffy know."

So we turned round and crept away and began the long journey back. Trying to think how we could give the news: the south was lost to us.

I said they were good at building things.

We took the news back as quick as we could. The wall was going up and there was no way back. The south was lost, so we looked the only way left to us: west. The only problem there was that soon we hit the sea. Beyond that, we knew, was a big island – tough land, not great, and not that many people. We thought – maybe if we could get there, they'd leave us alone.

I remember thinking how that would be nice. Me and Tella and Por, on a little farm somewhere. Tella would know what to do and we could learn. I was good at making bargains: there's a reason Kal would send me off on errands to the market, back in the old days, and I'd been the best scav around the Big Lock. We'd be fine. We'd be good. It wouldn't be grand, but we'd get by. As long as I didn't mind being the extra one, the non-essential one. The new Seffy and Crith, Kal had called them. Tella and Por. And me, tagging along, hoping as ever there'd be a few scraps of love left over. Hey, I'm not complaining; well, not much. Tella was so beautiful; Por was now so strong. They were the stuff that heroes are made of. What was I, really, in the great scheme of things?

So we pushed on west, towards the coast. It was nice to smell the sea again; smelt fresh, like freedom. I remember standing looking out, and turning to Kal, and saying, "Where's this island, then?"

She said, "You can't see it from the shore."

"Oh. So how do we get there?"

"How do you think? On boats."

"We don't have any boats."

"Quick, you, aren't you?"

"So what are we gonna do, Kal? Build 'em?"

"No."

"Why not?"

"No time."

"Then what?" I said. "What we gonna do?"

Her face all thin; her lips tight. "We pay our way over."

We'd carted money around right from the start, whatever we'd found in the old villas and homesteads that we'd passed through. Another thing Crith and Kal had argued about, back in the day. Crith said it would tempt people; they'd steal it and run away. She'd been right, a few had. Kal said we might have pay our way now again. She was right too. We'd bought some goods along the way. Now we took whatever was left over and hoped it would be enough.

There were free-traders schlepping up and down this part of the coast; hopping between the mainland and the island, and taking advantage of the fact that the masters' rule had been disrupted in this part of the world. I think a few people made a bit of money from that. So we thought, perhaps, they'd be... Well, not on our side, exactly, but mindful of the benefits they'd put that way. More fool us.

I don't know who did the deal with them. Kal? You'd think Kal was involved somehow, but if she was, the whole fucking mess that followed told me she was losing her grip. We were told to hurry, hurry – we couldn't hang around, had to get moving, on to a little bay were the ships were coming to pick us up. So we did, we hurried, and we got to the rendezvous. The ships came too – came right past. We watched them go right past. I heard later that whoever had struck the deal had handed over half the cash to secure passage, with promise of the rest after we were at the island. Well, that half was enough for those traders. Off went the ships, carrying half what we had, and we were left stuck on the sands, watching the tide go out. I always said that westerners were slippery bastards.

The Story of the Ship That Sailed Forever

Once upon a time there was a hand who was afraid of water. Now it is not a good thing for a hand to be afraid of anything, since more often than not we're asked to do all kinds of things that the masters want and they do not take much account of what makes us afraid, unless they think we are not sufficiently afraid of them. On the whole this was not a problem for the hand, since her master lived inland and her task was in the vineyards, and then one day she discovered she was being sold to a shipwright. How the other hands laughed to hear this! It is a sad truth about us that sometimes we make ourselves feel better by laughing at the misfortunes of our sisters, and that is only one of the mistakes that we make.

Well, the hand pleaded with her current master not to sell her, and promised she would work harder and better if only she could stay, but the truth was her master was not as wise as we would hope, and was very short of money. So the hand was sold, and bundled on the back of a wagon, and sent on her way to her new home.

She smelled the sea before she saw it, and she felt sick to her stomach. She heard the seabirds too, screeching and keening, and she stuffed her hands in her ears and tried not to listen. But the masters write our fates after all, and she could not get away, and soon enough she arrived at her master's factory. There she was set to work (she was good with wood), and her new master was very pleased with this purchase, and had no idea that each night the new hand wept at her fate, and cursed the hard world that had brought her to this place. And she became so desperate that she began to make her plan to get away.

Her master had taken on a new task, the biggest yet, and she was set to work upon it. It was to be the biggest, the greatest, and the most far-reaching ship that this hard old world had ever seen. And in a secret corner of this ship the hand built herself a little hideaway. Well, she was well aware of the joke of making her escape by ship, but she could see no other way, and she told herself that if she kept quiet in her little corner she did not need to see the sea, and even if she rocked about, she could tell herself that all she was feeling was the wind in the rafters of the old farmhouse where she had been born, and where her sisters still lived, whom she had never forgotten and never would, as far as she travelled.

At last the day came when the ship was to be launched. The hand, finding an excuse to be sent on an errand, in fact slipped away and on board the ship, and she went down to her little hideaway, and with nothing else to do, she fell asleep.

When she woke, everything was quiet. She could not feel the ship rocking, and she wondered whether they were yet at sea. She crept out from her hole, and went for a look around. And what a strange place the ship turned out to be, for it was full of hands, stowaways like her, creeping from their hidey-holes, and marvelling at the sight of each other. One of them said they should go up on deck, but they couldn't find a door, only a window. They all gathered round this window, and looked out. And one of them said, "That is the night sky." And another said, "Those are the stars, but they look strange." And a third, our hand, said, "That is the rock of the world, there, in the distance."

And they stood together, gathered round the window, and watched the old world hanging there. Then they set off to explore their ship. Every day, however, at the end of the day, they gathered at the window and looked back at the old hard world. And every day, it became a little smaller, until one day they could not see it at all. But by that time they no longer bothered to gather at the window, because they were so busy with everything else. And that was the end of that.

That is the last I have heard of the ship, and the hands that stowed away upon it. Their story has slipped away from me, into the darkness between the stars. I have heard no more news from it. I have never heard that this ship reached its destination. It left many years ago and has sailed off well beyond my knowledge. So anything I tell you now is not true, not as such, but what I think should be true, which is true enough in its own way.

The story that I like to tell is this: that the ship slipped the bounds of this old world, and sailed away into the stars, and it took the hand with it, took her off to worlds and places that we can barely imagine, except in our hopes and dreams. And maybe one day her ship will come to land, and she will climb out and set foot on a new world, or maybe it will be her children, or her children's children, or the children that come after that. On the ship sails, into the darkness, and it takes hopes and dreams and children with it, and we will never see where it comes ashore, but can only hope that it is a good land, and a kind land, far far from the rock of this hard old world.

Thirteen

It's hard to tell you this last part. Really hard. And not just because I didn't see the very end. Not that I'm disappointed about that, mind you. Who would want to see that?

So. Bits and pieces. The last part.

We'd played our hand, and someone was now pretty rich on the back of us – again – and yet we had won nothing. Worse. We were stuck with the sea behind us and a wall ahead of us and, for all we knew, the masters' armies getting ready to come through that wall and finish us off. We knew that a battle would do just that – we weren't the strength that we once had been.

Kal had one last plan up her sleeve. The general in charge of the wall-building was called Palliaire we'd learned, listening into their 'casts. Palliaire. Yeah, you know that name too, don't you? Glad to say things didn't end well for her, either. This is the thing with the masters. No matter how big you are, someone will be ready to kill you. Anyway, there was no love lost between her and Crassiaire, as everyone knows who has studied hard and learned the masters' history, and knows what came after all this, and as we knew at the time. Two generals, both looking for advancement. She sent a message to Palliaire, offering the rest of our money if she'd let us through and south. I know, desperate. You look at that offer and wonder what Kal was thinking. My guess is that money wasn't all that Kal offered. I think she offered herself and Seffy too.

Well, it wasn't enough, not by any means, and I don't think it would have been enough if we've had all the masters' wealth doubled and doubled again to offer. We couldn't be allowed to live free. They couldn't have that. So no deal. All that was left was to fight.

I noticed, over the next few days, because I'm good at noticing this kind of thing, that there were fewer little uns around. Fewer of us around my age too – friends, not best pals like Tella and Por, but people I knew well and got along with. Well, this sort of thing doesn't happen by chance and I knew to ask.

"Kal," I said. "Where are you sending the children?"

"I swear," she sighed, "you'll get yourself into trouble one day."

"Yeah, that ship's sailed. Where are they going?"

"Down the coast," she said. "Looking for some way across."

"Has it come to that?" I said.

"It's gone well beyond that," she said.

"Who's going to help them?" I said. "They robbed us."

"They just need a friendly face here and there," she said. "Someone with a little boat going over to the island who doesn't mind a little passenger or two."

"And when they're all gone?" I said. "When you've sent them off?"

"Then we turn back and face what's coming."

"All right," I said. "I'll try my best."

"Iss," she said. "You won't be in the battle."

"Eh?"

"Not you. You're going with the little uns."

"Oh, Kal, no!"

"I mean it. You'll be a liability. We'll spend too much time looking out for you –"

"Don't do this to me, Kal. Don't send me away, not now –"

She stepped forwards, and took my face between her hands. Not rough, mind you; the gentlest she'd ever been, if I think about it. "Now listen to me, you little bugger, and do what you're told for once in your life. I've not gone through all this to see you killed by those bastards. You'll go when I tell you and you'll get away and you'll live the best life you can, and every day you live beyond this, you're stealing from them, and you're giving me victory. Do you get it? You do what you're told for once and live."

Sometimes people have a funny way of saying "I love you", don't they?

"Do you promise, Iss?"

"All right. I promise."

"Head south and west. Get yourself over to the island. You understand?"

"Yeah."

"Good. Now bugger off. And send Por to me. I want a word with her."

The end came quicker than we'd anticipated, and the last of us had to go off in a dash. Por, at Kal's instruction, was heading off with me and the last of the little ones. She wasn't happy about that. But we were a bigger band than the rest, and Kal wanted a proper fighter with us.

Tella was going to the fight.

I didn't see their goodbye; of course I didn't. What I did see was Tella's blue goddess, tucked into Por's pack.

The night before, Seffy talked to us one last time. Tella and Por were together, lying on the ground, hand-in-hand. I sat down next to them, just a little to one side, and then before I knew it I was pulled towards them, between them, all our arms around each other.

"Hey, you lot," Seffy said. "We've come a long way together, haven't we? You know and I know it's coming to an end, so I'm not going to muck you around and say it isn't. But – oh stars! This time we've had! I wouldn't swap that for anything. Not for anything in the world. Tomorrow – it'll be bad, but it will come to an end. And some of us – well, maybe they'll live. Maybe they'll tell our story to whoever will listen. Tell about how we broke our fetters and turned the world upside down and saved our children, bright as stars and sweet as water."

I don't remember much of the rest of the night. We were heading off before dawn, anyway. I remember saying goodbye to Tella. Crying a lot. And then we went off, me and Por and a dozen others, creeping off into the darkness, hoping we'd pass unnoticed while the battle raged on behind.

That was the end of my time with the company. No, I didn't see the very end. Of course I didn't. If I'd been there, I'd've ended up the same way as the rest of them.

You know what happens. You've heard the end of this story. Seen it at the flicks, maybe. We lost, and those of us who didn't die on the day were coffled back north, and those who didn't die on the way were strung up along the road out from the capital. I hear it made quite a sight – some people even travelled to come and see. I'll never understand the masters. Anyway, that was the end of that.

The Greatest Story Ever Told

Here is a story, the best story. Once upon a time... No, wait, hang on, that isn't quite right, not quite. Once upon a time... Was that time in the past? Or is that time still going to happen? For what it's worth, I think it's both. History begins, and runs its course, and starts over, and round and round it comes again, and sometimes we are underlings and sometimes we are masters of our fates; sometimes we are powerless in the face of it all, and yet at the same time we *must*, we *have* to act...

Past or future, this story happens, has happened, will happen over and over again. That doesn't make it pointless, mind you. It makes it all the more precious. Every single time is precious, like a drop of water in a dry season, but it is precarious too, and time and grief and cruelty wear it away, until the next time.

Until the next time...

Imagine this – a whole bunch of people lived, once, or will live, or are living right now, who didn't like the way the world worked and tried to build a better one.

Perhaps they will run away to live in the greenwood. Perhaps they will creep about in fenland and strike against the invaders. Perhaps they farm dry land and will rise up against the law-makers, the road-builders, the masters and raisers of stone. Perhaps they are torn from their lands and forced into coffins ships and rise, rise up against the traders in flesh, the shacklers and fetterers and thieves. Perhaps they will steal a super-powerful vessel and escape to the stars. It is all of these, all of these at once. The stars will align, something will set in motion, someone will say: *Enough*... and it starts all over again, the fight, the dance, the levelling, the seizure of all that has been stolen and the making of the commons...

There is something within us that bends towards freedom and that will catch a sight of it wherever we are. The lunatic on the hillside hears it in the crack of thunder and sees it the lightning flash. The prisoner sees it in the dust motes twisting in the narrow light between the bars. It calls to each of us – the bright flash of the spring flower, the play of running water, the light of the sun and the moon and the stars, the sweet song of the bird over the muddy stalemate of the battlefield. It is there, within us all, waiting to be kindled, waiting to be coaxed to life.

Oh stars, oh heavens, let us swear upon the rock of the world that we will not sleep, we will not rest, until our children are restored to us, until the arc of history is bent right. We will rise up. We will rock the foundations of the world, and break our fetters. We will reach our hands up to the sky and capture the birds and cage them. We will take back our children, brighter to us than stars, sweeter to us than water.

Fourteen

So. That's how I got away, because the last thousand or so of us decided to make a stand and put themselves between us and the masters. We walked a very long way, through hard and empty country. The first heat wave came, so we were thirsty most of the time, and some of those little ones struggled. But the bigger ones – me and Por, three or four others – pulled them on. Carried them when we had to. Because we couldn't let them be taken. Not those little ones. Because we knew, I think, what the masters would be doing to the people they captured.

I think of them a lot, you know, hanging up there on them big forked logs. How can I not? I can't help myself thinking about things that aren't in front of me, never could. I'll be lying there thinking back over my days, all the years I've lived, and what else am I supposed to think about but the best time, but the best time ended in that... And I think of them there, up on those forked logs, and I start to think about what it must have felt like. You can last for days up there, can't you? Hanging there, trying to breathe, the weather turning hot the day after the battle – really hot. They must have been sweltering up there. Thirsty. Hurting. Listening to everyone else around them, in the same boat. Then, if they lasted that long, the smell... I don't know who survived the battle, you see. Seffy didn't, I think. Seffy went down in a blaze of glory, shining like the star she was, dancing to the last. Kal will have cut her own throat before getting that far. But what about Tella? What about my Tella, hanging there?

I heard that the masters filled every screen in every hall across the land with those pictures. Made sure every hand saw what would happen if they ever got an idea like that in their heads again. Well, I don't know if that's true or not, because at first I wasn't exactly popping out to the flicks, but mostly because I've never been near a picture hall since. The chance of seeing that? There's something about the flicks that makes everything more real, even though you know it's filtered and softened and ordered. There's something about it. I never want to see that. So that's that for me and the flicks. Funny, isn't it, what makes you angry? On top of everything else the masters took from me, I get so angry about

Una McCormack

that. I can't even go and stand there in the pit with everyone else, and let myself fade into that space. I loved the flicks. The masters have ruined even that. Funny what makes you angry, isn't it?

She was beautiful, Tella, you know. And by the end, she was so strong, so brave, so fearless. How I loved her...

Some people say you die before the day is over. Some people say it takes days to die. I don't know, people say what they want to hear, don't they? And I don't want to hear about that. I don't ever want to know.

Sometimes I think what it must have been like when Seffy went down. I see her as clear as if I'm there. She's standing there at the heart of the fight with all her enemies moving in towards her. I see her muscles tense, getting ready to kick to flick to dance. I see her stretch, stretch her hand up and out, to help to guide to lead.

I see the stars shine down on her and I hear her *laugh*... Because what else can you do, eh? What else does this hard old world let you do?

The masters say that when they die they go back to the stars. Imagine being able to believe that.

Well, listen to me, going on like this. You've been very patient, haven't you? I'm sure you've heard it all before, read about it maybe, or watched the story at the flicks. I suspect you've never heard it told like this, though. The masters have their own version, of course, all about how wild we were, how brutal. How we put kids in the front line so that the big ones could get away. How we killed half the south country and burned everything we saw. Yes, I bet we're a wild old bunch in those stories. A tale to tell your kids so they'll be afraid. So perhaps you haven't heard this before. How it was to be in the middle of things. I don't suppose there are many of us still around now, those kids who got away at the end. Twenty of us? Thirty?

No, I don't know what happened to them. This was a time to fade away, you see. My idea of a little house on the island, a little farm where we could live in peace – well, that was never going to happen. There wasn't strength in numbers, quite the opposite if you think about it. The masters had been plain enough, hadn't they, that they wanted us all dead, and we had no reason to disbelieve them. I suspect most of them found themselves hands again – there's safety, isn't there, in the life you've always known. I hope they haven't had sad lives, not too sad. Most of all,

I hope they haven't had cruel lives, or no more than the usual, the expected. No more than they were ready for. I hope they were small enough not to have come to expect better.

We got our party across the water to the island, and then we went off, in ones and twos, across the next few days. Made sure the smaller ones had someone with them. The last I saw of Por, she was walking down the coast path, holding hands with her little one. No, I never saw Por after that day. I mean it when I said I never saw any of them again, I'm not just saying that to protect them. I waited there until everyone was gone, and then I waited a few days more, and then I went on my way.

It wasn't that hard for me to blend in, which I think would have surprised Kal, given what she always said about my big mouth. But I'd got the hang of it during those months – had always had the hang of it, if the truth be told. Good at slipping away, hiding in quiet corners, making up a convincing story if someone ever caught up with me. The island was a quiet place, hadn't been touched by the trouble, as people there were calling it, and they weren't much interested in rights or wrongs of other people's business. There were hands here, of course, but not the big farms, and there was always work for someone else. So I made my way round the coast, down to the big port, and then I found myself a place on a boat, and I did that for a while. A long while. Got myself on bigger and bigger boats, until I almost lived on the water, went days and weeks without seeing land. Those big ships now, they're a sight to behold. The masters are clever, and they know how to make us work and build. They're good at getting things done, aren't they?

I worked down in the kitchens of those big boats, can you believe it? Came all that way only to find myself back where I started. Sometimes, I think this is the only way to find freedom. Find a crack somewhere, a small place, somewhere nobody will come looking, because it's too far away, or too greasy, or too grubby. People don't like to bother with those kinds of places. If you keep yourself busy, and do what you're told, and don't make a fuss, you can get by all right. Only sometimes I'd think of what else could have happened. If only we'd kept Crith, if only we'd taken the city, if only we'd been luckier or stronger or bolder...

Eh, though, those are stories for someone else. We gave it our best shot.

One day I didn't want to be on the water any more. So I came ashore.

I'd heard about the amnesty, of course, and I'd heard about manumission, and I sort of had a feeling that I'd qualify. I couldn't exactly say where I'd come from, and there were whole years I couldn't prove, but somehow I had enough of the right bits and pieces of paper. I walked into that office still a hand, and when I walked out, I was free.

Grateful? That's a funny thing to say. I suppose... I suppose in my head I was already free. I'd been free since that hot autumn day when I ran after the trucks and gave Kal lip, and the fighters laughed and took me as their mascot. That had never left me, even in that little boat as we crossed to the island. Besides, freedom isn't something the masters can give me, not really. Only in law, and I'm not a great believer in that law of theirs, because for years I stood outside. That's what a hand is, after all, someone whose life is not subject to the law. Someone who can be beaten, stolen, murdered. Someone subject to might, not right. So they didn't give me freedom, because that was there already. They put me within the law, that was all. Not that I'm complaining, mind you. When you get to my age, you take what you can get.

Fifty years since all this happened, more or less, and the world has changed beyond anything I might have imagined, even in those old stories of mine, and stayed some ways just the same. Yes, there was the amnesty, and yes, there was manumission for some of us, but there are still hands there, aren't there, born to it; and masters. Sometimes I think there will always be masters. Sometimes I have to make myself remember that there was a time when that wasn't true.

Is that the time? Yes, I know, I know, it's off soon, the ship that's heading to the stars. I'd like to have done that. Proper adventure. Those were my favourite stories, the stories of the journeys to the stars. And it's about time, isn't it? This world, now, it's getting old, and tired, dried up. So off we go, to find another world. They're good at big plans like that, the masters. They're good at getting big things done. They'll come down from the stars to another world, and bring their stories with them. The thing is – they'll bring us too, because they're nothing without us. And we'll take our stories with us: this one and a whole lot more. We are the rock the rock of the world the bones upon which everything rests.

About the Author

Una McCormack is a New York Times bestselling author specialising in TV tie-in novels. She has written novels, short fiction, audio dramas, and journalism for franchises such as Doctor Who, Star Trek, and Blake's 7. She is a lecturer in creative writing, and in 2017 was a judge for the Arthur C. Clarke Award.

NewCon Press Novellas
Set 3: The Martian Quartet

Cover Art by Jim Burns

The Martian Job – Jaine Fenn

When Lizzie Choi receives a message from her brother telling her that he's dead, she assumes it's a joke. By the time she realises it isn't and comes to understand what is being demanded of her, she's committed to taking Shiv's place in a criminal undertaking on Mars…

The pace never lets up in Jaine Fenn's The Martian Job, as pulp action SF collides with high concept science fiction, paying homage to classic movie *The Italian Job* along the way.

The Martian Simulacra: A Sherlock Holmes Mystery – Eric Brown

When the Martian Ambassador arrives at Holmes' door seeking the Great Detective's help in solving a grisly murder, how can he refuse? Ever since the second wave of Martians arrived on Earth, inoculated against the germs that had halted their tripods the first time around, and humanity accepted the aliens as their overlords, Holmes has been curious... Eric Brown delivers a glorious mash-up of Sherlock Holmes and *The War of the Worlds*, seasoned with a dash of *The Lost World* for good measure.

Phosphorus: A Winterstrike Story – Liz Williams

Winterstrike is at war. Even so, the last thing Canteley expects is for her mother to send her away in the company of her formidable Aunt Sulie, a member of the ruling Matriarchy, who wrap secrets around them as thick as winter snowfall. In *Phosphorus*, Liz Williams returns to the harsh Mars of her critically acclaimed novels *Banner of Souls* (shortlisted for the Arthur C. Clarke Award) and *Winterstrike*, delivering a tale laden with mystery and menace, as the Red Planet's bloody past and troubled present collide.

ORIGAMY
Rachel Armstrong

"*Origamy* is a magnificent, glittering explosion of a book: a meditation on creation, the poetry of science and the insane beauty of everything. You're going to need this." **- *Warren Ellis***

Mobius knows she isn't a novice weaver, but it seems she must re-learn the art of manipulating spacetime all over again. Encouraged by her parents, Newton and Shelley, she starts to experiment, and is soon travelling far and wide across the galaxy, encountering a dazzling array of bizarre cultures and races along the way. Yet all is not well, and it soon becomes clear that a dark menace is gathering, one that could threaten the very fabric of time and space and will require all weavers to unite if the universe is to stand any chance of surviving.

Rachel Armstrong is Professor of Experimental Architecture at Newcastle University and a 2010 Senior TED Fellow. A former medical doctor, she now designs experiments that explore the transition between inert and living matter and considers their implications for life beyond our solar system.

"*Origamy* crackles with a strange and brilliant energy, and folds the conventions of SF into beautiful new shapes. A rare and wonderful debut." **- *Adam Roberts***

"Perhaps the most astonishing and original piece of SF I've read in a long, long while." **- *Adrian Tchaikovsky***

"A visionary masterpiece. Science Fiction, Fantasy, science and poetry combine to create a lyric on life and death that spans the whole of creation. Delightful and mind-expanding. If you miss it you have missed one of the finest examples of literary art." **- *Justina Robson***

IMMANION PRESS

Purveyors of Speculative Fiction

Madame Two Swords by Tanith Lee

An unnamed narrator, in the French city of Troy, finds an old book of the writings of the revolutionary, Lucien de Ceppays, who lived and died in the city two centuries before. She feels a strange bond to the life and thoughts of this long-dead man – what is the mysterious truth behind her obsession? Perhaps she did not find the book at all – perhaps it found her. Some years later, impoverished after the death of her mother, the narrator – in a state of desperation – finds herself inexorably guided to meet the peculiar and unnerving Madame Two Swords, an old woman with a history, and her own enduring bonds to Lucien – as well as the book. For the narrator, reality seems to unravel, as she begins to penetrate just how intimately she is connected with Madame Two Swords and Lucien. Previously only available as a limited-edition hardback in 1988, the long-awaited new edition of this vintage-Tanith novella includes illustrations by Jarod Mills. ISBN 978-1-907737-81-7 £11.99, $15.50 pbk

Salty Kiss Island by Rhys Hughes

What is a fantastical love story? It isn't quite the same as an ordinary love story. The events that take place are stranger, more extreme, full of the passion of originality, invention and magic, as well as an intensification of emotional love. The stories in Salty Kiss Island are set in this world and others, spanning the spectrum of possible and impossible experiences, the uncharted territories of yearning, the depths and shoals of the heart, mind and soul. A love of language runs through them, parallel to the love that motivates their characters to feats of preposterous heroism, luminous lunacy and grandiose gesture. They include tales of minstrels and their catastrophic serenades, dreamers sinking into sequences of ever-deeper dreams, goddesses and mermaids, sailors and devils, messages in bottles that can think and speak but never be read, shadows with an independent life and voyagers of distant galaxies who are already at their destinations before they arrive.
ISBN: 978-1-907737-77-0, £11.99, $15.50 pbk

www.immanion-press.com